f l o o d

You told me to be
silent

flood

james heneghan

A Groundwood Book
Douglas & McIntyre
Vancouver Toronto

Groundwood Books / Douglas & McIntyre
720 Bathurst Street, Suite 500
Toronto, Ontario M5S 2R4

We acknowledge for their financial support of our publishing program
the Canada Council for the Arts, the Ontario Arts Council and the
Government of Canada through the Book Publishing Industry
Development Program (BPIDP)

ONTARIO ARTS COUNCIL
CONSEIL DES ARTS DE L'ONTARIO

National Library of Canada Cataloguing in Publication Data
Heneghan, James
Flood
ISBN 0-88899-466-4
Title.
PS8565.E581F46 2002   jC813'.54   C2001-903206-4
PR9199.3.H4496F46 2002

Designed by Barbara Grzeslo
Cover photograph: Darren Robb/Getty Images
Printed and bound in Canada

For Lucy, *mo grá*

Sheehogue (Celtic: rhymes with rogue. Also Sidhe, shee, sheoque, shihog, shee-og) n. 1 in Ireland, the faeries; the Little People. 2 the Irish faerie diaspora: faeries who left Ireland during the Great Famine and are now dispersed and scattered throughout the world.

—*Hughie Hoolihan's Dictionary of Irish Folk Lore*

PART I

the boy

1

IN THE SECOND AND THIRD WEEKS of September it rained almost every day.

The Sheehogue, fed up with the soggy North Vancouver Meadow, spent their days in the Muzak-filled mall practicing sundry small mischiefs. Giggling like wind chimes, they perched on the ledge of the automatic teller machine at the Canadian Imperial Bank of Commerce and caused people to forget their PIN numbers; they made the pampered lapdogs of elderly ladies neglect their hygiene etiquette in inconvenient places — elevators and richly carpeted fashion emporiums; they speeded up escalators, caused change to spill from purses, fur coats to leap at haughty customers, trays of chocolate pudding and soup to slide off restaurant tables, bursts of static to blast the ears of cell phone users.

Blame it on the weather, everyone said.

Then in the final week of September and the first week of October it rained nonstop every day. Things got serious. The Sheehogue gave up their pranks; life was no longer funny.

The Fraser and the Pitt rivers boiled angrily between their dikes as sandbagging crews worked around the clock. In the North Vancouver mountains the rivers and creeks swelled and burst their banks. Mosquito Creek went on a rampage, destroying a bridge before thundering over high walls of boulders and attacking a row of fine homes along its eastern bank.

The first thing the slumbering Sheehogue knew was the deafening boom that tumbled them from their grassy bowers. This was followed by a flood of water and mud over the meadow that swept the Sheehogue rapidly along in nature's unexpected waterslide. They saw the homes of mortals tumbling into the creek. "Save their children!" the Old Ones ordered.

In one of the houses not yet tumbled a boy sat up in bed, rigid with terror in the darkness. A woman screamed as the house shook and furniture crashed and pictures fell from the walls. Foundation timbers splintered. The boy fell from the bed onto the floor, then crawled on his knees to the door. He pulled himself up, struggling for balance against the tilt of the dying house, and stumbled out onto the landing, where the woman and a man clung together swaying on the stair, eyes wild. The boy reached for the woman. Plaster and debris fell from the roof.

"Out!" yelled the man.

The house was sliding. Water swirled through the

tilted hallway. The dark shape of the dining-room table leaned through the shattered window. The mud slide pushed the house off its foundation toward the roaring floodwaters. The three people were separated and swept away in a new rush of water into the dark current. They called to each other, but their voices were lost in the thunder of the avalanche.

The woman and the man were hurled downstream to where the floodwaters had torn a narrow suspension bridge from its moorings. Steel cables lashed wildly about like whips, cleaving the churning waters. Battered by the cables and leaping debris, the broken bodies of the woman and the man were thrown up onto what was left of the bridge, where they hung for a moment before being swept away to the ocean.

The boy, gasping for air, was borne along in the current closer to the bank. The Sheehogue pushed and shoved and ferried his battered body into the waiting arms of an uprooted cedar tree, where it remained firmly wedged, upside down, until a rescue team found it many hours later, in the afternoon.

He waited in Discharges, slumped in a green vinyl chair, head back, staring out the window at the foggy street. He was a small boy, thin and pale, with yellow bruises on his cheekbones and temples and around his eyes. Dark brown hair — almost black — flopped untidily over his forehead and eyebrows. His eyes, too, were a dark brown that in cer-

11

tain lights appeared black. He wore clothing provided by the hospital volunteers: blue jeans, white T-shirt, dark blue sweater, white socks, sneakers. A thin black nylon jacket hung over the back of his chair. He moved stiffly in the hard chair from the bruising on his arms, shoulders, and legs.

It was Friday. The clock in the nurses' station said it was twenty minutes after eight. He had been waiting more than an hour since his seven o'clock breakfast. The elderly night nurse had gone off duty. The day nurse was young. "I'll call the hotel," she offered helpfully. She found the number in the directory, dialed, and waited.

The boy stared out the window at the fog.

The nurse spoke into the mouthpiece, listened, and then put the telephone down. "Your aunt left an hour ago. She's probably delayed by the fog." She smiled sympathetically at the boy.

The boy said nothing.

The nurse brought him apple juice and a limp ham sandwich and some comics. He ignored the sandwich and comics but sipped the juice, holding the glass tightly and staring at the bilious green walls and at the top of the nurse's head bent over the desk behind the office window.

At nine o'clock, when the boy was almost asleep in his chair, a smell of fog and mothballs jolted him awake as a woman swept into the waiting room. She wore a gray overcoat that came to her ankles; tall and slim, she carried herself erect, with shoulders squared. A few strands of gray showed in her thick, severely cut black hair. She marched straight up to the boy. "You must be Andrew," she said briskly.

The boy stared into her dark, penetrating eyes.

"Well?" said the woman.

"Andy," whispered the boy.

"I'm your Aunt Mona, your mother's sister. I've come to take you home."

Andy said nothing.

She stood, inspecting him. "You're a Costello right enough," she said at last, "like me. You don't take after your father. Thank goodness," she added. She spoke in a nasal accent with a flat "ye" for you, and "muther" for mother, and had a grim, humorless face; the way she said "father" made it sound like a curse. And she still hadn't said how sorry and sad she was that Andy's mother was gone, the way the priest and the nurses had. Instead, she appeared rigid and tight, with her pale pinched face, as if she were keeping something frightful in, afraid it might burst out. She turned away from him and rapped impatiently on the window with something hard — a coin or a key. The nurse hurried to the counter.

"I am Mona Hogan. I'm here for my nephew."

The nurse pushed a paper across the counter for her to sign. Mona Hogan peered shortsightedly at the paper, snapped open her purse, took out a glasses case, put on her glasses, and read impatiently.

Andy stared out the window once more; the thick fog outside mirrored the way he felt. Except for the nightmares, he couldn't remember much about his first week in the hospital. But by the second week he was lucid, and Father Coughlan from All Saints' told him that his mother and stepfather were dead, drowned, God rest their eternal souls, and that his aunt was coming to take him back to Halifax with her, and was there anything he could do?

Andy could not believe his mother was dead. Clay maybe, but not his mother. How could she be dead? She had always been there for him. But the priest seemed to believe, so Andy asked him, "Can you bring my mother back?"

The priest shook his head sadly.

"Can you stop my aunt taking me to Halifax?"

Again the priest shook his head.

"Then there isn't anything you can do."

At night, when everyone else was asleep, he thought about his mother and wanted to cry but couldn't because he didn't want to believe that she was dead and if he cried that would be the same as believing it.

He now watched his aunt sign the paper with a quick scrawl, whisk off her glasses, return them to their case, close the case with a snap, drop the case into her purse, and snap the clasp closed. Snap-snap.

The nurse handed Aunt Mona a copy of the paper. Then she flashed Andy another sympathetic smile. "Goodbye, Andy. Take care of yourself."

Andy picked up his jacket and followed his aunt along the corridor. He had no bag, no belongings.

Outside he merged with the fog; he felt hollow and light, as though his interior geography consisted only of thin ribs arching about empty spaces. He was in the world again, out of the hospital, moving jerkily in a different medium from the one he'd left, like a swimmer emerging from the sea.

When they were both seated in the back of the taxi, Aunt Mona leaned forward and snapped "Air Canada!" at the driver.

The mothball smell off his aunt's gray coat penetrated the enclosed space of the taxi. Andy sat still, hands clenched together in his lap, remembering his mother, comparing her to this starchy woman who seemed so cold and so much older. His aunt's flat nasal accent was undoubtedly Irish, for his mother's family was Irish, he knew that, all born in Ireland except for his mother, who was born in Halifax.

Andy decided that he did not like his Aunt Mona very much, didn't like what his eyes could see, hadn't liked her from the beginning, when she'd looked down at him with stern black eyes, thin hands ungloved and clasped, body straight as a pencil, shoulders stiff, saying "your father" as if he'd committed a murder.

They drove along Marine Drive toward the bridge. Aunt Mona said, "You don't say much."

Andy stared out at the fog.

"You're eleven, right?"

He feigned deafness.

"You're small for your age."

He didn't need to be reminded that he was small; he already knew that, thank you very much. He glared at his aunt. She stared back at him. Her dark eyes seemed as

15

impenetrable as the October fog that surrounded them. Gray hat, gray skin, gray coat; if she stood outside in the fog she'd be invisible.

"Your mother was much younger than me, only a slip of a girl — barely nineteen when she married your father — and twenty-one when she left Halifax to come here with him. You were a baby, barely walking."

Andy stared out the window.

"Does your father ever write to you?"

"Huh?"

"What am I saying! Doesn't Vincent Flynn think only of himself. He wouldn't lift a finger to write a letter to Pontius Pilate if it was to save Jesus Christ Himself."

"My father is dead."

"Stuff and nonsense! Children should not be told lies."

Andy pushed his hair out of his eyes. "It's not a lie! He died in the war."

"Judith told you a lie. For a good reason, I'm sure. Your mother meant well. But the truth is all we have, child. 'Turn your horse off the path and be caught in the bog,' my father used to say."

Andy wanted to say, You're the liar, not my mother! But he didn't say it; he said instead, "My father died in the war. He was a hero."

Aunt Mona gave a sniff and tilted her chin.

Andy said nothing more as he stared resolutely at the cars passing foggily by in the other lanes, his jaw muscles clenched.

Finally Aunt Mona said, "Hero is as hero does. Believe

what you like, but Vincent Flynn is alive and large as life, walking the streets of Halifax, and was never in any war. There was a time, when I first knew him, when he might have been a hero, but he threw it all away. There. Now you know. That's the truth of it. The only war familiar to your father is the one he fights to pay for all the Guinness and whiskey he drinks, and to find money to throw away on the gambling. God knows I'm not one to lie. And I'm not an uncharitable woman. But he dragged you and your mother off to British Columbia and never did a day's work once he got there. After years of poverty and heartbreak, your poor mother finally came to her senses and threw the rascal out. You would've been only five or so. Your bold father came running back to Halifax like a rat to an old but sure ship; there's the brave hero for you."

"He's really alive?" Andy felt a heart-jumping rush of excitement.

Aunt Mona shrugged. "I've not seen the scoundrel in years — nor do I want to — but the last I heard, he was living in the north end, sitting every afternoon and evening with his degenerate companions in Dan Noonan's pub. Either he's there or he's in jail."

Andy drew a deep breath. His father alive! He was finding it difficult to breathe.

"Vincent Flynn would charm the birds off the trees. If anyone ever kissed the Blarney Stone, then it was himself. Except for six or seven months in the brewery, where he met your poor mother, Vincent Flynn never did a day's work in his life. It grieves me to say it, but he was once a man who could've been anything he wanted, but he threw it all away for the drink. And now he's nothing but a waster and a thief."

They drove along in silence for a while, Andy thinking furiously. He stared at his aunt's hands on her lap; they were a bloodless white with prominent blue veins, the fingers like the slender votive candles in All Saints' Church. On one of the fingers she wore a plain gold ring.

"He was a gambler and a drunk. Your mother was a blind fool to put up with him for so long; nobody was surprised when she finally threw him out. She was better off without him."

Silence.

Aunt Mona turned her head. "D'you remember him at all?"

Andy made no answer. He could not remember his father's face, for that had faded and his mother kept no pictures of him, but he remembered his voice, or thought he did, telling him stories of the Faeries, or the Sheehogue, as he called them.

"Judith was better off without him," Aunt Mona said again. "Good riddance to bad rubbish!"

Andy sat quietly, the hatred for his aunt circling the emptiness inside him and scraping the bony arc of his ribs. He examined her again out of the corner of his eye: the frowning, worried face; the thick black hair with its few gray strands, short, barely covering her ears; the thin pale lips, bare of lipstick. He turned away and closed his eyes.

His father alive! And all these years he had thought

him dead. But he wasn't dead: he was alive, in Halifax. The hatred for his aunt was temporarily forgotten as thoughts of seeing his father began to fill his emptiness and he felt a new sense of purpose. He straightened his shoulders. He was leaving Vancouver, British Columbia, the only home he could remember, and he was setting out for Halifax, Nova Scotia, his birthplace.

Where his father lived.

Aunt Mona sat upright in her seat, peering ahead into the fog. They drove over Lions Gate Bridge, rising in a vaporous arc above the waters of Burrard Inlet. The fog was thicker here. The traffic crawled. The haunting moan of the nearby Prospect Point foghorn was answered by another far away along the coast at Lighthouse Park. They sounded like two lonely creatures of the fog calling to their lost child.

A small Sheehogue work party accompanied the boy in the taxicab, sharing the empty seat beside the driver. They had saved a life. They had a responsibility. It was customary.

2

"HOW WILL WE GO?" they asked the Old One.

"Wherever the wind blows, so go we," the Old One answered.

"But this is the airport!" protested a Young One.

"And that's an airplane!" said another, pointing out to the tarmac.

"Yes."

"So what's all this 'wind blows, so go we' stuff?"

The Old One sighed. "Air Canada is quicker."

They checked in at the airport, made their way to Gate 2B, then sat side by side, not looking at each other, waiting for their flight to be called.

Aunt Mona said, "Last night I went to your house — or the place where it used to stand, more like. Afterward I talked with your parish priest, Father Coughlan."

She had arrived in Vancouver yesterday afternoon. Why hadn't she come to the hospital to see him? Andy wondered.

As if she had been reading his mind, she said, "I was unwell. I checked into the hotel and then tried to see you. Children's visiting was over at eight. I was too late. They said you were sleeping."

Aunt Mona was a witch, Andy decided.

He noticed her hands trembling. From the cold? But the lounge was warm. Old age? Not yet; she wasn't an old lady like his friend Ben's grandmother; Aunt Mona was quite a bit older than Andy's mother but she wasn't really old, not like she was going to keel over and die any minute, and her hair was still black, and she walked like she had lots of energy, even if she was a bit stiff in the neck and shoulders. She had mentioned being unwell, meaning what? A head cold? Flu? Stomach upset?

Aunt Mona said, "I had a call from your stepfather's lawyer. We had a long talk."

She was talking about Clay. Clay had owned a software business. Now he was dead. Andy felt nothing about that; but the thought of his mother squeezed his heart.

"The lawyer said the flood was an act of God," continued Aunt Mona, chattering mechanically as though now she'd started she couldn't stop. "Floods and earthquakes and landslides, that kind of thing," she said, as if talking to herself, "are acts of God, which means you're not covered by insurance, not usually, unless ..."

Her voice ran on. Andy's head ached. He closed his eyes. He didn't want to hear any of this. His mother was gone, missing, and nothing was left: the house, the ground it had stood on, the cars in the garage. Everything, everybody, gone, swept away, leaving only a hole in Andy's heart.

Aunt Mona's voice droned on. There might be some money coming from his stepfather's life insurance policy, she said, and if they were lucky there could be some from a government flood relief fund. Insurance would be paid on the two cars. But altogether it didn't sound as if it would be very much; it would do no good to get their hopes up; they would have to wait and see.

So that was it, thought Andy. The old witch was expecting to collect on the house insurance. Served her right there was none. Money was the reason! Money was why she had come three thousand miles to Vancouver, not to rescue Andy and bring him back safely to the place of his birth, as she'd told the hospital and Father Coughlan over the telephone. It was for the insurance money. He might have guessed as much. His aunt was a phony. Andy wasn't a baby: he was eleven years old — eleven and a quarter, to be exact. There had been no need for sweet, kind, considerate Aunt Mona to go to the expense and trouble of coming all the way to the West Coast for him. All she had to do was send the ticket and Father Coughlan would have made sure he got the right flight.

Old witch.

The hatred flooded his arteries and swamped his heart.

They sat together in the crowded airplane, Aunt Mona with her hands clasped in her lap, head back on the headrest, eyes closed. Her breathing seemed harsher; her hands trembled more than ever.

"Are you all right?" asked Andy.

"Of course I'm all right," she snapped without open
her eyes.

Old cow.

Andy dozed fitfully most of the way, uninterested in
the movie, waking only to eat and drink. His aunt seemed
to be sleeping, too, eating nothing, drinking only water for
the entire flight, refusing offers of meals and snacks from
the busy flight attendants.

At one point when Andy woke up, he saw threaded
through his aunt's thin, trembling fingers a string of rosary
beads. Her pale lips moved silently in prayer. Andy hated
people who prayed in public. He thought maliciously: she
wants people to think she's good, but I know better: she's
an evil old witch.

In his periods of wakefulness, Andy's mind replayed
images of the flood, and he remembered his helplessness,
and the noise and the hurt of it. Broken bodies. Death.
Images of his mother and Clay, the house and school,
friends, soccer. He would miss the other kids on the team.
And he would miss soccer; he was one of the school's best
players, tops at dribbling the ball through several defend-
ers and then driving it into the goal. He was soccer mad,
his mother said. He followed soccer on TV, had taped the
men's World Cup last year, and most of the women's this
year. The Canadian women's team wasn't good, but they
had tried their best; the winners, the U.S.A., were an
astounding team and deserved to win. He'd seen the
women's final live on TV. China was a great team, too,

and so were Brazil and Nigeria. Andy's mother had worried about him watching so much women's sports. "But they're just as good as the men," Andy had tried to explain.

He'd kept a small library of videotapes in his room, tapes he'd made of important soccer games mostly, but there were circus tapes, too, of trapeze artists and animal trainers with lions and tigers and bears; the tapes were gone with everything else.

He planned to be a professional soccer player when he grew up. He would be famous and play for Manchester United or some other top European team, and he'd play for Canada in the World Cup. His second choice of career was circus and movie animal trainer; his third choice, trapeze artist. He had discussed the subject with his mother, who thought that a career in soccer might be best, as it was possibly a little safer than the other two choices.

He stared out the window at the thick white clouds below the airplane, wondering about heaven. That was where the priest said Andy's mother was. And the nurses. Your mom and dad are in heaven, they said. He didn't bother explaining to the nurses that Clay was only his stepfather and he wasn't too worried whether he was in heaven or not. Aunt Mona had said nothing about his mother being in heaven. Maybe she didn't believe in heaven. Maybe there was no heaven. But if there was no heaven, where could his mother be? He hoped she was all right. He felt like crying. Maybe if he searched in the clouds he might see her signaling that she was all right.

He kept looking out at the clouds, but his mother didn't appear.

He felt tired, sleepy. It was the first time he had ever been in an airplane. Hundreds of people propped up in seats sleeping, talking, watching a movie, reading, using the washroom as they were borne through the thin air with no sense of speed, flying so high in the sky that nobody on the ground knew they were there, a separate hidden place between the earth and the stars.

The flight attendants, the ones Andy could see working in his area, seemed to be having trouble pouring drinks. Passengers were being dumped on accidentally. A couple in the seats ahead, who had been arguing quietly ever since they got on, had tomato juice spilled over them. The P.A. chimed oddly, like bells in the wind, and the captain came on to apologize for troublesome air pockets and the P.A. acting up.

The five-and-a-half-hour flight seemed to take forever. It was evening, Halifax time, when they arrived. Aunt Mona became more and more grim. They were both exhausted and had nothing to say to each other.

A bus took them from the airport to the city. "Follow me!" said Aunt Mona briskly in her no-nonsense voice, clambering down from the bus with her carry-on bag. She staggered and almost fell, but managed to right herself. Her face was very pale. Like death warmed over, Andy thought nastily.

"Wait up," said Andy, pausing on the bottom step of the bus. He pointed to the candy machine in the bus depot. "Could I get some gum?"

Aunt Mona reached into her bag and with trembling fingers handed him a coin from her purse. "Be quick." Andy took the money. Aunt Mona dropped her overnight bag on the ground and waited, hands on bony hips, head back, breathing deeply, as though unable to inhale enough of her home air.

Andy looked at the bus driver. He had a pale face and slicked-back hair, and wore a dark jacket with a monogram on the pocket. He was watching Andy with a great deal of curiosity, as if he had guessed what he was about to do.

Andy hurried quickly past the candy machine, and then, without pausing to see if his aunt was watching, fled out the door and into the thick gray brawl of the city.

They tumbled off the bus in surprised disarray. Even the Old One had been caught napping. The Young Ones tittered disrespectfully. They followed the boy, the speed of their going blowing the hats off the heads of the bus drivers and swirling a litter of dirt, newspapers, and gum and candy bar wrappers high in the air in whirlwinds of dusty confusion.

"Hurry!" the Old One called. "Hurry, hurry!"

3

HE RAN AWAY FROM HIS AUNT as fast as his weak, tired legs would carry him.

The Halifax streets were shrouded in a gray fog almost as thick as the one he'd left behind in Vancouver. Was the whole country covered in an October fog, then? He listened for the moan of a foghorn but heard only the roar of traffic and the monotonous barking of a dog tied to a bicycle stand outside a convenience store.

He was alone.

What if he got lost?

"Lost" was his most unfavorite word. LOST. The thought of it shot sharp arrows through him. Lost was being alone and not knowing the way home. "Alone" was his second most unfavorite word. ALONE. Alone could be dangerous. The word echoed hollowly in his head like a stone booming in a well. He couldn't be lost and he couldn't be alone. He had been only too aware of this when deciding suddenly to run away from his aunt: it had not been easy.

He *had* to find his father! His father was alive. Vincent Flynn was alive in the north end, in Dan Noonan's pub. But what if he wasn't in Dan Noonan's pub? Then surely Mr. Noonan would know where he lived.

His father was no thief, Andy was certain of that. What had she called him? A waster? Aunt Mona was a nasty old woman, vicious and jealous. She hadn't seen Andy's father in years, her own words, so what could she know of him!

Shoulders hunched, hands pushed down into the pockets of his thin jacket, he hurried, heading anywhere as long as it was away from the bus station and his nasty gray aunt. He glanced behind often, searching the faces, afraid his aunt might be following, or had sent the police after him. There was no way he wanted to live with that mean old woman. No way. He would find his father and they would live happily ever after, end of story.

He crossed the busy street in the middle of a block, heading for a group of teenagers clustered together outside a coffee shop. The traffic was crawling. He dodged between the cars and trucks. There were four kids watching him approach.

"Could you tell me how to get to Dan Noonan's pub?" He directed his question at the tallest boy in the group, a skinny, ginger-haired kid, probably about fourteen, in a torn jeans jacket.

"Huh?" The boy looked cold. He frowned and sought help from his friends. "D'y'know that pub?"

The boys shook their heads.

"It's somewhere in the north end," said Andy.

"North end?" said a boy with a shaved head. He wore a ring through his lower lip. He pointed to a high clock tower. "Fifteen-minute walk. Up the hill and past the Citadel."

"Thanks," said Andy.

Shaved Head asked, "What happened to your face?"

Andy hurried away without answering.

He walked and walked. He was tired; his whole body ached. Just when he thought he would have to give up, he found it in a narrow dirty street; a streetlight shone on NOONAN'S PUBLIC HOUSE in peeling red capitals over the pub's green exterior. His heart lifted.

He pushed through double doors into the bar. The place was crowded and he had to burrow his way in like a rabbit, through clothing that smelled of sweat, beer, and cigarette smoke. He looked at the men. Any one of them could be his father. A small piece fell out of his heart at the thought of it. There were two men working behind the bar. To make himself heard above the sounds of TV and drinkers, he raised his voice so that he was almost shouting.

"Who?" asked one of the bartenders, craning his neck at him and pulling a pint of beer at the same time. The beer was black like used car oil, with a creamy foam at the top.

"Vincent Flynn," Andy repeated.

The bartender put the beer up on the counter and looked around the room. "I don't see him." Andy watched the creamy foam spilling over the rim of the glass. "It's early yet," said the bartender. "Come back later, I'll tell him you were askin'. What's your name, kid?"

"I'll come back." The bartender knew Andy's father. He wasn't dead, killed in the war; his aunt was right; his father was alive and close by. Andy felt his belly churn with excited anticipation.

Outside, a chill wind had come up, clearing the thin fog. Andy could see the glow of light from the distant clock tower. He fingered his aunt's dollar in his pocket. His jacket was too thin to keep out the cold. He shivered. Two weeks in the hospital had weakened him. His legs felt wobbly. But they knew his father, they knew Vincent Flynn. This was the place. Soon he would meet him!

There were very few people in the street. He rested, massaging an aching shoulder, leaning his back against the wall, figuring what to do next. Find someplace warm. He pushed himself off the wall and headed toward a lighted restaurant, passing people who seemed to drift along with wavering liquid steps, as though walking on the bottom of the sea, eyes staring, arms, shoulders, and thighs pushing against the weight of deep water.

The restaurant was shabby but warm. People, men mainly, sat about on cracked yellow plastic chairs, smoking cigarettes and sipping coffee under harsh fluorescent lights, elbows leaning on chipped Formica tables. Most stared vacantly with fish eyes at their coffee mugs or at the wall. A woman wearing high heels and bright red lipstick moved about in a friendly way talking to the men. One man was eating a hamburger and another was writing in a notebook. The smell of bacon and fried onions reminded Andy that he was hungry. He had eaten the meals on the airplane, the chicken and vegetables and the bits of fruit in their tiny plastic cups and the thin crackers and bread-sticks freed from cellophane wrappers, but now he was hungry again. And cold.

He clutched the money in his pocket and entered the restaurant. He ignored the food and asked for a cup of tea; it would warm him up.

"Help yerself," said the woman behind the counter, nodding toward a box of tea bags and a stack of shiny metal teapots.

He helped himself to tea and lots of milk and sugar and held out his dollar. The woman took it, returning no change.

He found a seat at the end of a table, empty except for the old man writing in a notebook. The man looked up, squinted at Andy through his cigarette smoke, and slid closer. He tapped his notebook with nicotine-stained claws. "I'm writing the history of the great hunger of '47," he croaked. "A thousand pages it'll be altogether when it's finished."

Andy looked at the man's book. The handwriting was neat, tiny capitals, every inch of the page filled with it. The old man's lips — he had no teeth — collapsed and sucked around the cigarette stub. He spoke out of the side of his mouth. "What's your name?"

"Andy."

A small, thin man in a giant's raincoat came over and said to the old man, "How're your cigs, Barney?" As he spoke, he looked over the old man's head at Andy and smiled.

"Gimme wan," croaked Barney, reaching into the pocket of his torn coat, extracting a handful of change, and handing over two dollars.

The man reached into a large, specially made pocket inside his raincoat and handed Barney a package of cigarettes, laughing and joking at the same time. Andy could not follow what he was saying, but when he'd finished, Barney was laughing loudly and hoarsely, and started a coughing fit that caused the cigarette seller to thump him helpfully on the back until the old man had recovered his breath.

"You'll be the death of me, so you will!" spluttered the old man, a wide gummy grin on his face. The cigarette seller moved on to the next table.

Andy finished his tea and left.

Noonan's was a fog of thick smoke. Andy pushed his way up to the same bartender. "Did he come in?"

The bartender's forehead was slicked with sweat; he shook his head. "I was looking out for him, but he hasn't set a foot inside the door."

"Do you know where he lives?"

The bartender shouted across to a man wearing a cloth cap, "Eamon? Where does Vinny Flynn live?"

Eamon shouted something.

"Mayo Rooms," said the bartender. "It's up beyond the cemetery. Turn right out the door and keep going. You can't miss it — the old building on the corner."

When he got outside, it was starting to rain. He pulled up the collar of his jacket and set off on weary legs to meet his father.

the father

4

THE BUILDING WAS OLD AND SHABBY. The name MAYO OO s hung above him in the rainy darkness in peeling green letters, the marooned o's a pair of spooky black spectacles watching him.

The lobby was empty. Silent. He made his way down a narrow hallway, his wet sneakers squishing quiet prayers on the worn linoleum floor. The faded green wallpaper was stained and torn in several places. A sign on one of the doors said, JOHN ROONEY, MANAGER. He knocked on the door.

Silence.

It was late; perhaps the manager was in bed. He knocked again, louder this time.

"Coming, coming." A woman opened the door. She wore a faded pink terry-towel robe over her nightgown.

"I'm looking for Vincent Flynn."

The woman was old, with tinted hair so wispy thin she was almost bald. She peered at Andy's face with milky eyes. "Mother of God! Who beat you, child?"

"It was an accident."

The woman pointed a crooked finger at the stairs. "Twenty-four."

"Thanks."

The old woman watched him climb the stairs.

On each stair he said a prayer.

Smells of mildew and decay, stale cigarette smoke, fried bacon. He was trembling. He stood outside 24, listening. No sounds within. He knocked and waited. Nothing. He knocked again. He could hear the rattle of a truck as it bounced and splashed over a pothole outside in the street.

He tramped back down the stairs. The woman had closed her door. The hall was empty. He heard a toilet flush. An old drunk hobbled in from the street, came up to Andy at the foot of the stairs, and put out a hand, attempting to stroke Andy's head. "You're a fine young feller," he mumbled. "Come to keep an old man company, have ye?"

"Leave me alone!" Andy flung the man's arm away.

The man staggered backwards, almost falling, blinked blearily at Andy, then suddenly zigzagged away toward a room at the back of the building, screaming, "Ow! Stoppit! Oooh! Ow!" as if being kicked by demons.

Down the hall, a toilet flushed again.

Andy was tired; he wanted to put his head down and sleep, but no, he was near his father. It wouldn't be long now. He could stay awake.

He waited outside on the street for a while, but it soon became too cold, and he returned to the inside and sat on the stairs. He could not keep his eyes open. If he fell asleep in the hallway, the police might find him and take him back to Aunt Mona. Under the stairs there was a closet for housekeeping equipment and supplies. It smelled of cleaning fluid and a hundred years of dust and dirt. He crawled in and closed the door. Darkness. Nobody would find him here. He wasn't scared of the dark, he told himself. There was nothing to be frightened of; only harmless brooms and mops and plastic bottles of solvents. Nothing to be afraid of. He lay down on the hard floor and closed his eyes. Soon he would meet his father and he wouldn't be alone. Forget alone: think father, father, repeating in his head like the steady drip of a faucet. He could hear the buzz of a TV from the manager's room, like a bluebottle fly on a window. He was exhausted. He wasn't afraid. He fell asleep.

He awoke with a start, not knowing where he was in the darkness of the closet, thinking he was in the hospital. There were sounds outside of people moving about. Voices. Noisy boots and shoes climbing the stairs over his head.

Then he remembered. He was ALONE in a hole under the stairs. He had to get out. Acid burned in his stomach as he ran his hands frantically over the door, found the latch, pushed the door open, and peered out. The hallway was empty. Stiff and sore, he crawled from the closet, wobbled his way out to the street, and sucked in a lungful of cold air. He guessed the time to be well after midnight. He went back, climbed the stairs, and stood outside number 24. He took a deep breath to still his leaping heart and knocked on the door.

Nothing. He knocked again, louder this time, and was startled by a sudden burst of wild laughter from within. The door was jerked open.

An ugly, bearded man with an enormous belly said, "Howyeh?" He had a cigarette burning in the corner of his mouth. When Andy made no reply he said, "You looking for someone?"

Don't let this man be my father, he prayed.

"Vincent Flynn?"

The man stared at him. The cigarette was burning very close to his beard. "He's busy."

"Who is it, Cassidy?" a man called.

Another man shouted excitedly, "Two bucks on Black Beauty!"

The fat man, Cassidy, turned and yelled into the room, "It's someone for you, Vinny." He turned again to Andy. "You might as well come in." He stepped back, holding the door open.

Andy stayed where he was.

"Come on in," Cassidy urged. "Vinny won't bite you." He laughed at his own joke. "Hey, Vinny, it's a wee lad."

Andy peered around Cassidy's belly. The room was foggy blue with swirling cigarette smoke. Four men were kneeling on the floor, passing around a bottle of liquor, their attention on five huge black cockroaches scuttling and scrambling inside a miniature arena formed from cartons of cigarettes. It was a game. Five small piles of bills and coins lay on the floor. There were several ashtrays with cigarette stubs and burnt matches.

On the word "lad," one of the men stood and faced Andy, regarding him quizzically.

Andy recognized him immediately. It was the skinny little man in the giant's raincoat who was selling cigarettes in the restaurant. He had watery blue eyes, and with his raincoat off he looked even skinnier than before.

"I'm looking for Vincent Flynn."

The cigarette man replied with a happy smile, "You're looking at him: Vinny Flynn at your service."

The Young Ones were already restless and homesick. "The boy looks after himself very well without us," they grumbled in the ancient tongue.

"He has found his father," said another. "The boy is safe."

"Not yet. It is too soon. We must wait and see," said the Old One.

"We could be home having fun," they complained, "playing with the traffic lights on Georgia Street."

"Snarling up the middle lane of Lions Gate Bridge."

"Crashing disk drives."

"Jamming revolving doors."

"Losing socks."

"Credit cards."

"Car keys."

"Wait and see," the Old One said again.

5

THIS MAN WAS HIS FATHER? Andy stared at the cigarette man for the longest time, unable to speak. Finally he said, "I'm Andy."

Vincent Flynn smiled at him.

"I'm Andy Flynn," he said again. "Your son. From Vancouver."

The cigarette man's eyes widened in surprise. "Andrew?"

"Andy."

"Is it you? I don't believe it!" He looked outside, down the hallway. "Where's your mother?"

"She's ... gone."

"Gone?" The cigarette man's face fell. "Holy Mother of God! You don't say? Judith? How ... ?"

The cigarette man really was his father: his mother's name on his lips made it true. "There was a flood ... the house ... everything."

His father stood staring, as if his shoes were nailed to the floor, as if he were seeing a ghost.

One of the men yelled, "Hey, Vinny, are yiz in for this round or what?"

Vincent Flynn half turned. "I'm … out," he stammered. He hadn't taken his eyes off Andy.

They stared at each other. "Come in, come in," the cigarette man said at last, holding the door open for him to pass.

Except for his small size, Andy could see nothing of himself in this man who was supposed to be his father. Aunt Mona was right: there was very little resemblance. His father's eyes were pale blue, for one thing, not dark like Andy's and his mother's and Aunt Mona's. He had long, untidy ginger-brown hair with gray in it, and a tired, narrow face that needed a shave.

"Place your bets, ladies and gentlemen!" called one of the players on the floor in a phony French accent.

Aware of his father's eyes greedily drinking him in, Andy shyly turned away and watched the game. One of the men inverted a mug in the center of the cigarette carton arena and shook the black insects out onto the floor. Long antennae probing the air ahead, they scuttled quickly for the darkness at the edges of the cigarette carton walls. The men whooped and cheered. "Show 'em the way, Gertrude!" yelled the fat man, Cassidy. "Move it, baby!" yelled a second man with a foreign accent. A third man, wearing a dirty khaki baseball cap with *Pumping Iron Gym, New York City* on the front in red and black, was speechless as he leaned over the arena wall, his eyes wobbling with excitement, and the fourth man, no teeth, only bare gums, screeched loudly like an owl, "Hoo-hoo, hoo-hoo!"

The cockroaches crawled, wandered, scrambled to within an inch of the outer finishing circle, but in a sudden and most unusual move that astonished the onlookers, about-turned abruptly and sped back, side by side in a straight line, toward the center. On reaching the center, they turned again and crouched, perfectly still, antennae poised, as though awaiting a starter's gun.

"I never saw anything like it!" said Cassidy.

Like racehorses at the starting gate, the black insects suddenly exploded into life and made a direct sprint for the finish.

"Did you ever see such a thing?" screeched the tooth-less one.

"Black Beauty it is!" yelled the man in the baseball cap. He twisted around to look up. "Hey, Vinny! Did ye see that? I never saw the likes of it in all my life!"

Vincent Flynn stopped staring at Andy and turned to his friends. "Out, fellers! Game's over! All of yiz out!" He started snatching things up off the floor, pushing at the men, hurrying them. "Move it, boys!"

One of the men, the quiet one with the baseball cap, scooped the writhing insects up in his cupped hand and emptied them into a jam jar, capped it with a lid, and thrust the jar into his jacket pocket. Cassidy swigged back the dregs and dropped the empty bottle onto the sofa. The men grabbed their money and hurried to the door, stuffing bills and coins into their pockets. Cassidy stopped and looked back. "Hey, Vinny! See you later at you-know-where, okay?" He gave a wink. The latch rattled as the door closed, and then there was silence.

Vincent Flynn said, "Andrew!"

"Andy."

"Andy is it now? I can't believe it's you I'm looking at!"

There was that smile again, in a friendly, open face. This was the man who, according to his mother, was killed in the war, but who, according to Aunt Mona, had been kicked out by his mother when Andy was only five.

"Sit down, why don't you," said his father — his dad — waving toward the sofa, "while I take a good look at you."

Andy sat. His father started tidying up, throwing the cartons of cigarettes from the cockroach races onto the sofa, grabbing and snatching at litter, ashtrays, glasses, rushing them out to the tiny kitchen, moving quickly, smoothly.

Andy watching him, felt suddenly exhausted. He'd slept only a short time, two hours, maybe not that, in the broom closet.

When Vincent Flynn had finished tidying, he grasped the bottom of the window and jerked it open to let out the smoke. Then he sat on the arm of a shabby easy chair, facing Andy. "The bruises," he said, peering closely at Andy's face, "are from the flood, then?"

Andy nodded. There were so many questions he wanted to ask, but fatigue silenced him. Instead, he looked more closely at his father: he wore a plain green cotton shirt under a blue ribbed sweater, worn brown cords, and a pair of shabby brown shoes. The sweater had food stains down the front. He looked again at his open face: pale watery blue eyes, smiling mouth; recalling the warm, welcoming voice, the accent so much like Aunt Mona's, he didn't find it hard to believe that this was the same voice of the Little People tales when he was little.

And yesterday he hadn't known his father was alive.

Vincent Flynn sprang from the arm of the chair and made as if to throw his arms about Andy, but then stopped and gripped his hand affectionately instead, as if unsure of how long-lost fathers greeted long-lost sons.

"Andy!" he cried enthusiastically. "These old eyes are delighted to see you!" He perched himself opposite on the arm of the chair again, hands on his knees, nicotine-stained fingers drumming, eyes dancing with excitement. "All grown up! How old are you now? Ten is it?"

"Eleven."

"Of course, eleven. And the fine young man you are. I wouldn't have known you. Pinch me and tell me you're really here, that it's really yourself I'm looking at." He bounced up again and grasped both Andy's hands and crushed them in his own.

Andy felt overwhelmed. "It's me all right," he said weakly.

"You're tired. Why don't you take off your things and lie on the sofa. I'll bring a blanket."

Andy was relieved to slip out of his jacket, kick off his wet sneakers, and stretch out on something soft.

His father pulled off his damp socks, threw a blanket

over him, and switched off the light. "I'm dreadful sorry about your mother. It's a terrible thing. We'll have a good chin-wag in the morning," he said. "Will I close the window? Is it too cold?"

"It's okay." At least his father had said something about his mother, that he was sorry she was gone, a terrible thing he'd called it, which was a lot more than Aunt Mona had said.

"Sleep tight. If the Sheehogue come creeping through the open window and bother you, just give me a shout and I'll send them on their way."

The Sheehogue. The Faeries. Andy smiled.

And fell fast asleep.

" 'Gallop apace, you fiery-footed steeds.' "

"You cheated!" they said, giggling.

"No I didn't." The Young One laughed and turned her back on her accusers.

"Yes you did. We saw you sprinkle St. Patrick's wort on your beast's antennae as we all raced together, we saw you, we saw you, we saw — "

"I did no such thing! It was only a dab of shamrock powder for the smell."

"I slipped off at the start," said another. "Or I would have won, I'm sure, St. Patrick's wort or not."

"Roaches give off very little smell. Unlike horses."

"The roach is much faster than the horse, pound for pound."

"But not as reliable."

"Nonsense! I traveled the length of the Grand Canal from Dublin to Tullamore one moonless night in a roach and coach, and there's no better beast in all ..."

"I'd rather ride a rat than a roach," said a Young One who had contributed very little to the discussion so far.

"Are you out of your mind entirely ... ?"

They squabbled noisily.

"Enough," said the Old One, hiding a smile.

6

"DID AUNT MONA come looking for me last night?" asked Andy the next morning as soon as his father appeared, emerging sleepily from his bedroom in blue polka-dot boxer shorts. "I thought I heard you talking to her out in the hallway."

"Don't worry; I didn't let her in."

"She wants to take me away."

"Yes."

"You won't let her, will you?"

"Of course not. You're safe with me, my boy. She might as well try rob the Bank of Canada as steal you away from your own loving father, and that's the truth."

He searched his father's eyes and saw that it was indeed the truth.

"Where's the bathroom?"

"Across the hall. It's shared." He scratched his skinny bare chest.

The bathroom door was locked. Andy was about to turn away when he heard the toilet flush and the bolt rattle. He stood back as the door opened. An old man with a walking cane limped out slowly and hobbled past him without a word. Andy watched him climb the stairs that led up to the third floor, hanging on to the banister for support.

Andy went in and switched on the light. There were no windows. The place smelled bad. There was a dead cockroach lying on its back in the tub. The toilet seat was dirty. There was no way Andy was going to sit in that tub. Or wash in that filthy basin. He didn't need to wash, he decided.

When he got back, his father, now in the same clothes he had worn the day before, was making tea. "An old guy from upstairs left a mess in the bathroom," said Andy.

"Carried a cane? Bald as an egg?"

"That's him."

"Old Peter. He's supposed to use the toilet on his own floor, but if there's someone using it he can't wait; the poor man has his problems, right enough. Do you want some tea?"

"Tea's fine."

There was nothing for breakfast. "All I have mornings," his father explained, "is a cup of tea." Daylight, uncombed hair, and ginger stubble gave his thin face the look of an old man's. He shuffled back and forth between the kitchen and the table. "Tell me about your poor mother," he said, sitting at the table with two mugs of tea, pushing one toward Andy.

Andy sat. "The flood took the house away. We were in bed. And Mom …" He stopped.

"Judith was a fine woman. May she rest in peace."

"What does 'rest in peace' mean? Is she in heaven?"

His eyes shone with tears. "Poor Judith," he said, shaking his head.

Andy waited. Then he said, "Clay is resting, too. In peace. He was my stepfather."

"God save him."

"Do you think Mom is in heaven?" Andy asked again.

His father couldn't answer. His eyes were full. After a while he said, "God save them both," and sat, shaking his head over his tea, talking about the random cruelty of nature and a whole bunch of stuff Andy couldn't understand. Andy drank his tea and stared at the man opposite him, wishing he would talk about the place where his mother was, whether she was happy there, whether she could see them sitting and drinking tea together, whether she was really dead when Andy felt she was still very much alive, and what did she think of Andy living in Halifax with this odd, untidy man who was once her husband?

When his father finally stopped talking, Andy said, "So you're my real father."

"I'm your father, right enough, though you'd never know it, looking at the pair of us. You're a fine boy. You're like the Costellos, the dark chocolate eyes and hair the color of soot." He smiled. "Your mother's family. They came out from Ireland. Your Aunt Mona was only twelve. That was a year before your mother was born."

The mention of Aunt Mona prompted Andy to ask, "What if Aunt Mona sends the police for me?"

"I'm your father, Andy. You're safe here with me. Don't worry."

"You won't let them take me?"

"Never, as long as I draw breath into this miserable body."

"I hate her."

He leaned forward and placed a hand over Andy's on the table. "It's sometimes terrible hard to love everyone, son, the way it tells us in the good book, but not hating comes a little easier. Hate will twist your soul if you let it, Andy. Hate no man or woman, you hear me?"

He nodded.

His father started a rambling talk again, this time about Judith's family, how they left Ireland for Canada many years ago, and the troubles they'd had, but Andy hardly listened, letting his gaze explore the room. If he didn't count the tiny kitchen, not much bigger than a closet, it was really just two rooms: this small living room, almost bare, with plain, dirty walls in need of fresh paint, and a door leading off into his father's bedroom. The only furniture was the torn brown sofa and the faded green chair, probably rescued from a garbage dump by the looks of them, and the small wooden table at which they sat near the window. There was a saucer in the center of the table containing a few raisins. Their two chairs were scarred and cracked. A *Playboy* centerfold was taped to the wall near the kitchen. There was nothing else. No rug or carpet on the torn linoleum floor, no other pictures on the walls, no TV, no radio, and no telephone that Andy could see. The room had only one window; its ragged, smoke-stained curtains hung uncertainly on a few remaining hooks. The place had the sour, musty smell of stale food and smoke. A yellow nylon rope stretched across one corner of the room with a pair of tartan boxer shorts and a pair of grayed white socks hanging from it.

"I can see that you don't think much of the place."

Andy shrugged.

"It's enough for me. I'm not in it much." Vincent Flynn looked around and, seeing the centerfold as if for the first time, got up quickly and tore it down.

Andy pretended not to notice. "How come you're not working today?"

He laughed. "I'm not working because I've no job, that's why. There's no work to be had, and brutal unemployment all over the province."

"You were selling cigarettes in that restaurant last night."

"I was, indeed. These uncertain times force a man to turn his hand to low employment."

"Why do you sell them so cheap?"

"Because they're cheap cigs. I buy them from the wholesalers, old stock, stale and out of date. I get them for next to nothing." He sighed. "It's a way of surviving."

Andy remembered what his miserable old aunt had said about Vincent Flynn being a thief. Nasty old cow. His father worked hard selling those stale cigarettes.

"I thought to myself, when I saw you in the restaurant, Andy, that there was something about you, and I'll swear I felt a thump right here." His hands went to his thin chest. "I should've known it was my own flesh and blood I was looking at, my own dear boy. I'm so astonished to see you, Andy. How on earth did you find me?"

Andy told him about Aunt Mona coming for him and how he had run away.

His father laughed with delight at his daring and urged him to tell more.

"I slept downstairs in the broom closet."

"You're the brave one; a young lion, so you are. Take after your father, you do. Mona went to fetch you from Vancouver, is that right?"

"Yes."

"Well, I never." He shook his head in disbelief. "She told me nothing. I hadn't seen the woman in years. Which reminds me. What day is this?"

"Saturday."

"D'you like hockey?"

"You bet!"

"The Mooseheads are at Metro Centre this afternoon."

"You mean real live hockey? Not the TV?"

"It's the only kind."

Andy was delighted. Clay, much too busy with his business, had never had the time to take him anywhere. Clay didn't like kids anyway. Andy had overheard him admit as much to one of his friends over the telephone when he thought nobody else was listening. And his mother had no interest in hockey — besides, she'd always been busy with her Robson Street shopping and her friends and her tennis and her aerobics classes, not to mention her personal trainer who took her running most days.

His father rinsed the mugs under the tap, then dropped a piece of soap into his mug and began mixing lather with a shaving brush. Andy watched him pulling faces into a small cracked mirror over the sink as he scraped his chin with a safety razor, rinsing the lather off every few seconds under the tap. "I usually wash here in the kitchen," his father explained when he'd finished. "Saves walking down the hall." He handed Andy a towel that looked much used. Andy stared at it. "I need to buy a few things," his father admitted, embarrassed.

Andy said nothing. There was a piece of soap on the lip of the sink but no toothpaste or extra toothbrush. His father said, "You're welcome to use my toothbrush. And look, I use baking soda, see?" He handed Andy a package. "Better than toothpaste."

"No thanks."

"I've got an old one you could have if you like. It's clean, nothing but baking soda was ever on it."

"Thanks anyway."

He cleaned his teeth with his fingers. Then he leaned over the kitchen sink and threw some water on his face and dried it off. The sink was small, cracked, and yellowed. To the side of it there was a dirty hot plate and an old iron frying pan; a small fridge sat on a counter opposite.

They boarded a bus outside the Mayo Rooms. Vincent Flynn wore his old raincoat, its inside pockets bulging with cigarettes. There was a big crowd at the Centre. The music was loud. Andy followed his father as he pushed his way through the bodies to join a mob of screaming kids who were already high-fiving the red-green-white-uniformed players as they came onto the ice. The Mooseheads were playing their provincial rivals, the Cape Breton Screaming Eagles. The noise was frantic. There was a pause in the music while starting lineups were announced.

Vincent Flynn seemed to know everyone, laughing and joking as he sold his stale cigarettes. As soon as the game started he said to Andy, "Stay right here. I'll be back in a jiff." He disappeared into the crowd of spectators. He was away longer than a jiff, whatever that was, but Andy didn't mind; he was with kids his own age, and the game was as riveting as soccer, especially with the addition of noise — music, yelling and cheering, the clatter of hockey sticks, collisions against the boards — as well as the smells of clothing and food, all absent from TV games. There were exciting moments when the puck disappeared and they had to bring on a new one. It happened several times after a knot of players converged on the puck, slicing away at it, banging their sticks together, shoving and shouldering, then disentangling themselves and gaping at the ice in astonishment when there was no sign of the puck.

Later, on the bus home, Andy noticed that the bulges in his father's raincoat had disappeared. The bus was full. He sat close to his father, feeling the warmth of him. The passengers were hockey fans in Moosehead caps and thick parkas; many wore gloves, and scarves in the Moosehead colors. Again, his father seemed to know everyone.

"This is my kid from Vancouver," he said, putting an arm around him. "My son, Andy."

"Didn't know you had a kid, Vinny," someone said.

"Well, now you know. Aren't I the lucky man?"

"Welcome to Halifax, Andy," another man said.

His father told a joke to the two men in the seat ahead. The men laughed. The men in the seats behind and to the side were leaning over, listening to his father begin a joke about Sherlock Holmes and Watson on a camping trip. When he'd finished, the laughter drowned out the noise of the whining transmission as the bus labored up a hill amid the roar of traffic.

His father was fun. Andy couldn't for a minute imagine him complaining about Andy's clothes, as his mother sometimes did, or about his junk food habit or muddy shoes or the way he bit his lip when he was worried. But now he was with his father, laughing Vinny Flynn, who wore an old raincoat with pockets the size of shopping bags, and shabby brown shoes, who seemed happy living in a run-down rooming house with no proper furniture and no comforts, who was in business for himself selling stale cigarettes, and who spent his money betting on cockroaches. Andy's mother and Clay had had everything: clothes, fine house, expensive furniture, cars, but were they as happy as his father? Andy wondered now. When was the last time he'd heard his mother laugh, really laugh? No: Vincent Flynn had to be the most exciting, interesting person in the whole world. And he was Andy's father.

All the seats were taken, so the Old One settled himself on the luggage rack and closed his eyes. The hockey game had worn him out.

"It was so exciting!" The Young Ones were thrilled. They swung on the overhead handrail, laughing and chattering like monkeys.

"Show us the pucks you stole."

"I didn't steal them. Borrowed, that's all."

"We could start a league in the meadow!"

"We could carve hockey sticks from fir or hemlock."

"Pine's better."

"Not at all. Willow's best."

"Hickory or ash. Hardwoods. Everyone knows that."

They squabbled for a while, then appealed to the Old One, but he was fast asleep.

7

BACK AT THE MAYO ROOMS, Andy's father hung his raincoat on the back of the door, then stood stiffly to attention
in the center of the room, facing the window, with his feet
together, arms straight to his sides, eyes fixed on the ceiling. "Shoulders back, feet together, arms at the sides, and
begin on the right foot," he intoned seriously. He advanced
his right leg stiffly forward, toes pointed like a ballet
dancer's, and then, as though stung by a bee, started hopping and leaping like a man made of rubber to the music of
his own voice, his hands never leaving his sides, his feet
flashing out and his knees jerking up and down like a pup-
pet's. "With a da-did-de-da-da-diddle-diddle-dum-dum," he
sang.

Andy laughed at the sight of his father dancing. He sig-
naled for Andy to join in, but Andy shook his head, suddenly shy.

His father finished the dance with a loud hoot, collaps-
ing breathlessly onto the floor.

"Are you all right — Dad?" asked Andy, testing the new

name, but was so unused to the word that it felt like sand on his tongue. He had never called his stepfather Dad or Father or Pop or any of those kinds of names, just Clay or nothing at all. Calling this crazy man Dad was going to take a bit of getting used to.

His father filled his lungs with air, puffing and blowing and laughing. "I'm not as young as I used to be," he gasped.

"Is that Irish dancing?"

"It is. Ah! You should have seen me when I was alive."

Andy laughed. "You're still alive. But you shouldn't smoke."

"I shouldn't; you're right. But I'm too old to give it up. Set in my ways I am, Andy darlin'. Here, help me up. Set in my ways."

Andy gripped his father's hand in both his own and helped him up and watched him while he sat on the sofa, out of breath, exaggerating his condition by blowing out his cheeks and rolling his eyes as though about to expire on the spot.

"Ah! It was at the ceilidh dancing I met your mother, God save her. Those were the days, when we'd dance the whole night long. Judith was the great little dancer, so she was. She'd lepp all night if she was let."

"Aunt Mona said you met Mother in the brewery. She worked in the office."

"Mona was only half right. I looked for her in the office every morning as I clocked in. The men were not allowed to speak to the office staff unless they were spoken to first, but I'd give her a sly wink and she'd smile or blush. Then one night she was at the ceilidh, and that was the first time I ever spoke to her."

"What did you say?"

"I asked her for a dance, of course. Then I told her I was bursting to speak to her, waiting for over a month with the words itching and fidgeting inside me, but now that I had her in front of me, eye to eye, I didn't know what to say except she was the prettiest girl I'd ever seen and the finest dancer in all of Halifax."

Andy smiled. "What did she say?"

"She thanked me for the compliment, but I could see she wasn't won over right away by my charm and good looks. I was only a little feller, y'see — not the powerful giant you see today." He chuckled. "And there were lots of big strapping lads after her. It took a while for her to go out with me. Persistence pays off. Faint heart never won fair lady, my daddy used to say as he led with his strongest trump — he was a great cardplayer, my daddy."

Andy cut through his father's confusing babble. "Why did you leave us?"

"I'll make us a drop of tea."

It was as if he hadn't heard the question. Andy followed his father into the kitchen, and while his father was filling the kettle and rinsing the teapot, Andy opened the fridge: empty except for a small carton of milk, a bowl of sugar, half a bag of potato chips, and a package of raisins. He took out the milk and sugar for the tea and the chips and put them on the table. Next he opened the top drawer near the kitchen sink: the inside was dirty; it held only a few knives, spoons, forks, can opener, bottle opener. Mrs. Morton, his mother's cleaning lady, would have a hemorrhage if she saw this place.

They sat drinking their tea and sharing the potato chips.

"You must have the bedroom tonight," said his father. "I will sleep in here on the sofa."

"No," said Andy. "The sofa's fine for me."

"Just for tonight, then. Tomorrow I'll find you a proper bed." He frowned.

Andy felt a niggling doubt. "You do want me, don't you, Dad — living here with you, I mean?"

"Of course I want you!" Raised eyebrows, eyes widening. "Aren't you my own darlin' son. When I lost you I cried so hard it rained in Nova Scotia for a whole year without a stop."

"Did you really miss me? All those years without me, I mean?"

"It was like I'd lost an arm and the use of my legs. I missed you something dreadful. Many's the time I'd sit at this very table nursing a mug of tea in these poor hands. And I'd think of you far away in that awful rainy place and I'd wonder what you and your mother were doing, and I'd feel dreadful lonely, and I'd say a little prayer that someday I'd bring you over here, back to Halifax, the place where you were born." He shook his head. "Miserable I was. I even thought of going back to Ireland, but I didn't, for then you'd be lost to me forever. It's terrible about your mother, but it's brilliant that you're here. Have another drop of tea."

Andy held out his cup and his father poured. The place was cold. There was no heater of any kind in the room. But the tea was hot. He folded his hands around the mug. His poor father didn't have much idea of how to make himself comfortable. Andy would have to help him make his life better.

His father sat smoking. "Help yourself to milk and sugar."

Andy tried again. "I was only five years old, just a little kid, when you left."

His father sighed. "Not much more than a baby."

"Why did you leave?"

"What did your mother tell you?"

"She said you died in the war."

"What war was that, I wonder? But reports of my death have been greatly exaggerated." He chuckled as he helped himself to more tea and stirred in milk and sugar.

"Well?" Andy intended to keep after him until he had some answers.

When his father saw how serious he was, he fixed his pale eyes on him. "I didn't run away and leave you, Andy. I'd never do such a thing, may God strike me down this very minute if I'm telling a lie. The fact is, your mother, the saints preserve her, wanted shut of me, and that's the truth. With no proper job and no prospects, I was no good to either of you. A terrible husband and a poor father. Your mother craved a comfortable life. And she deserved it. She made a mistake marrying a nobody like me, should've married a man with plenty of money."

"She did. She married Clay."

"I am happy she found the right man."

"But why didn't you write to me? Or send a birthday card? You could've done that at least."

Vincent Flynn shook his head. "I was never much good at the writing and the reading." He laughed. "I was the only kid in Dublin ever to fail kindergarten."

"But you can read, can't you? And write?"

"Aye, but very poorly, I'm ashamed to admit."

"There's no need for you to feel ashamed, Dad. Lots of people don't read so good. It's nothing." Andy touched his father's hand sympathetically.

Andy settled for the night on the sofa.

His father said, "I'm away out for a couple of hours. Will you be all right if I leave you?" His raincoat pockets bulged.

"I'll be fine."

"I must see a man. He's expecting me. Are you sure you'll be all right?"

"No problem."

"I'll lock the door as I go. Keep it fastened. Let no one in." He switched the light off at the door as he left.

Andy wondered whether he should get up and turn the light on again. It was scary being alone in the dark in a strange place. But he wasn't a little kid anymore — he was eleven; he needed no light. He'd had a little orange night-light in his room in Vancouver, with another outside on the landing so he could see his way to the bathroom, though he hadn't really needed them. Had he? No, not really. He closed his eyes and huddled down under the blanket, a lonely ache pulling at his heart as he thought of his mother, who wasn't in the room next to him where he could call to her. She wasn't in the next room; she wasn't even in Halifax, she was ... How could that be? How could you be living your life, every day pretty much the same as the day before and everything normal and going to school and weekends and playing soccer and suddenly it was all changed and the mom you saw every day — who bugged you about chores and about the mess in your room and the way you slouched instead of walking straight and the way your nails were bitten down to nothing, and when will you stop biting your lip like that every time I look at you, and I'm not your slave at your beck and call every minute, and I've stitched the button back on and folded all your things and put them in your drawers, and you look quite nice in that sweater, brown looks good on you, goes with your eyes, and sometimes I'd like for just you and me, Andy, to take a cruise somewhere, Alaska maybe, would you like that, just the two of us? Not this summer, though, too many things to do, but we'll do it before you're much older, I promise, just the two of us — when the mom you saw every day was gone, too late, Mother, you gone and only me by myself in this cold room and everything changed.

He was cold. He wondered if there was an extra blanket in the bedroom, but didn't get up to search.

He was almost asleep when a knock came to the door.

"Who is it?" Heart jumping.

"Vinny?" A man's voice, harsh and impatient.

Andy got up. "He's out," he called through the door.

The man clumped away down the stairs.

Andy groped for the light switch. His fingers found it. The naked bulb hanging from the center of the ceiling lit the room poorly, but it was enough for him to see the swarm of insects — cockroaches. There must have been hundreds of them, all sizes from tiny brown to huge black, fleeing from the light back to their nests behind the baseboards. In the few seconds he stood frozen with horror at the door, and before he could move, they had all disappeared into cracks in the walls. His chest thumped as though he'd rushed up twenty flights of stairs.

There were more of them in his father's bedroom when he switched on the light, swarming at the edges of the baseboards. He watched them scurrying for cover and waited until they'd all disappeared, then searched for an extra blanket. There was no closet, only an old chest of drawers. He pulled the drawers open. His father's worn and faded shirts and underclothes were crammed in untidily. He found an old wool blanket, thin and gray, under the chest, and carried it gingerly to the other room and shook it vigorously, looking for cockroaches. He was starting to shiver with the cold. With a cushion for a pillow he tried to make himself comfortable again on the sofa. He hadn't switched off the light: the thought of cockroaches scurrying about the room in the darkness and climbing up onto the sofa while he slept gave him the shivers.

Had cockroaches crawled over his unconscious body downstairs in the broom closet?

He tried to put the cockroaches out of his mind, but it was difficult. He thought about what people in Vancouver would be doing right now. They were four hours behind. Ten o'clock in Halifax would be six in the evening in Vancouver. Rush hour. Gridlock on Lions Gate Bridge. His friends at Monteray Elementary School would be having their supper. It was strange to think of it being suppertime there when it was bedtime here. Did Ben miss walking home from school with him? How many other kids had lost their homes in the flood? He didn't know, hadn't thought to ask in the hospital. He and Ben had usually walked home together down the steep hills and past the impossibly steep driveways to Ben's house, where they usually said goodbye, leaving Andy to angle over to Canyon Drive and walk along the path above the creek alone. The creek that had changed and become a killer. He thought about the flood and the hospital, his mother dead. Clay gone, too. Why hadn't Ben come to see him in the hospital? Maybe he had, but Andy couldn't remember. Nor could he remember if he'd seen other flood survivors in the hospital. The two weeks were an almost blank slate. He remembered his face in the bathroom mirror, though, when he first saw the bruises, the eyes unnaturally large and black, remembered the priest coming one afternoon to tell him that his aunt was coming from Halifax to take care of him.

And now here he was in Halifax with the cockroaches.

His eyes searched the floor, expecting to see them, but there were none; the dim light was enough to keep them in their holes.

Vinny. Lord of the roaches.

Vinny was a funny name. But it suited him.

He closed his eyes. He mustn't call him Vinny, even to himself; he was his father, after all; he would soon get used to calling him Dad.

Could cockroaches sense when a person was asleep? Would they come out of their nests into the light? He opened his eyes again and peered at the baseboards. Nothing. He closed his eyes again.

It would take a powerful lot of getting used to, living with cockroaches in this small bare, cold place after being accustomed to his own clean, warm room in their big house, the kitchen of which had been bigger than the whole of Vinny's — Dad's — place. But he was with his father, his real father, not Clay, and he was funny and great and Andy was glad he'd run away from rotten mean old Aunt Mona to be with him.

His belly hurt. He suddenly remembered he was hungry. They hadn't eaten much all day, just the tea for breakfast, and a bag of caramel corn at the game, and tea tonight, with a few stale potato chips. No wonder his father was so thin, living on tea.

He tried to forget about cockroaches and food and eventually fell asleep dreaming of skating with his father and the Mooseheads, and scoring the winning goal, and his father laughing and dancing and slapping him on the back and them both eating a jumbo-sized pizza, tomato sauce smeared over their happy faces.

The Young Ones were homesick for their meadow. One of them said, "Surely we can go. The boy is safe. What harm can come to the wee lad with his own father taking care of him?"

"There is nothing more we can do here," agreed one of the others.

"The father is not too bad a dancer," said a Young One who sometimes had difficulty following arguments.

"There's more to happiness than dancing," said the Old One.

"But the boy is safe now," the Young Ones chorused.

"Perhaps. We'll wait and see," said the Old One.

8

HE WOKE IN THE NIGHT and wondered about the time. The place was quiet. And cold. The light was still on. He scanned the floor and baseboards. No cockroaches. He got up and crept over to his father's room and looked in. Empty: he hadn't returned home.

He was hungry. He looked in the fridge but saw only raisins and the usual stuff for tea. He finished off the raisins and went back to bed but couldn't sleep knowing he was alone. With only cockroaches to keep him company, he lay on the hard sofa, wrapping the blankets tightly around himself to keep out the cold, trying to sleep.

But it was no good. He got up again, watching for cockroaches, and went to the window and tugged at the bottom, opening up a narrow gap. It was raining. The place was icy and silent and scary as a graveyard. He climbed back into bed, trying not to think of screamer films: a kid or woman alone in a dark place; horror; evil forces outside preparing to break in.

Someone was coming up the stairs. His heart started

racing. He sat up, the blankets pulled about him. Key fumbling in the lock. Of course! It was his father coming home. But what if it was someone else? He waited, muscles tensed, ready to leap and run.

The door opened and his father came in backwards, holding the door open with foot and elbow and dragging a large cardboard box. Andy was so relieved to see him, but before he could say anything his father had left the box near the table and gone out again. A few minutes later he came clumping up the stairs with another box, which he dragged in and stacked on top of the first. He locked the door, and then saw Andy clutching the blankets and staring at him.

"It's only me, Andy. Go back to sleep now, there's the boy." He patted Andy's head gently, then glided past him into his own room and closed the door.

When Andy finally fell asleep, wrapped in blankets like a larva in its cocoon, it was to the persistent but comfortable sound of the rain drumming on the fire escape and the comforting knowledge that his father was home.

He woke to the sound of loud thumping on the door.

Daylight. He sat up, rubbing the sleep from his eyes. There were two large cardboard boxes near the table that weren't there last night. And then he remembered his father coming in late.

The heavy thumping came again.

His father appeared in a panic, in tartan boxer shorts, hopping on one bare foot like a circus clown, trying to get his second leg into his trousers, almost falling. He hopped over to the window, pulled up his trousers, and jerked the window wide open. The rain blew into the room, fluttering the grub-by curtains. The room couldn't be any colder if it were in the Arctic.

The thumping came again, louder, rattling the lockworks. A man yelled, "Open up, it's the police."

The police! They had come to take him back to Aunt Mona.

His father grabbed the top box and thrust it out the window onto the fire escape.

"Open up!" The man was trying to kick in the door with his boots.

His father frantically pushed the second box out onto the fire escape, then closed the window and hurried to answer the door.

Two plainclothes policemen pushed their way into the room and immediately started searching. Vincent Flynn lounged in the easy chair and yawned, and scratched his skinny bare chest, watching them unconcernedly. "How-yeh?" he asked them.

The men ignored him.

"It's dreadful early to be waking people up," said Vincent Flynn, "but I know what it is to be a public servant doing his unpleasant duty. Somebody has to do the dirty work so we law-abiding citizens can sleep safe in our beds, even on a Sunday. I'm a great supporter and admirer of the police. Tell me what it is you're looking for and I'll help you find it." He yawned elaborately, threw one leg over the arm of the chair, and leaned back, stretching, yellow nicotine nails scratching at his unshaven chin and untidy mop of ginger-brown hair. "It's not that old biddy downstairs complaining of the dancing on the floor, is it? Nellie Doyle has no appreciation of the dancing arts. Doesn't she drive me frantic with her constant complaining."

One policeman, slow and ponderous, black mustache, looked in the kitchen while the other, wearing thick glasses like the bottoms of Pepsi bottles, quick on his feet, disappeared into the bedroom.

Andy noticed that his father hadn't drawn the curtains; he could see the edges of the boxes out on the fire escape. The policemen were sure to see them. Suddenly there was a brisk wind and the curtains closed with a snap. Andy blinked in astonishment.

"You were seen, Vinny," Glasses shouted threateningly from the bedroom, "so it's no use denying it."

"Where are they, Vinny?" Mustache growled as he came back into the living room.

"They're right here, boys," said Vincent Flynn cheerfully. He got up and went to the kitchen and brought back a bottle of whiskey. He put the bottle on the table.

The two policemen stopped searching and stared at the bottle of whiskey as if it were the Koh-i-noor diamond.

Andy's father went back to the kitchen and fetched three glasses, which he put on the table beside the bottle. He slowly poured an inch of whiskey into each of the glasses.

The policemen hadn't taken their eyes off the whiskey.

In a calmer, quieter voice, Mustache said, "You and Cassidy were seen hanging around Maloney's warehouse, Vinny." He removed his cap, smoothed his hair, put the cap on again, and reached for the whiskey.

"Maloney's was broken into last night," Glasses said quietly as he took the glass from Vincent Flynn's outstretched hand.

"Maloney's is it?" said Vincent Flynn, his blue eyes wide with innocence. He raised his glass. *"Sláinte."*

The policemen raised theirs. *"Sláinte,"* they murmured in unison.

"Old Maloney has things awful hard," said Vincent. "With all that money weighing him down and a wife with a tongue on her like tripe in vinegar, there's no wonder he's always in the sunny Carribean away from it all. And you poor fellers out in the cold rain on a Sunday morning looking after his money for him; my heart bleeds for yiz. The life of a guard is terrible hard — there's the poet coming out in me — don't I know it well, having been a military man myself. But you're mistaken, boys, if you think it's meself who was at Maloney's, for I didn't budge out all night." He turned to Andy. "Did I, Andy?"

The two men turned and looked at Andy as though seeing him for the first time.

Andy clung to the blankets, wishing the men would go.

"Och! I didn't introduce you to my son!" said his father proudly. "This is Andy, my own flesh and blood, dear to my heart. With his midnight hair in sweet disarray and the face of a sleepy-eyed angel, isn't he the finest young lad you ever saw? I'm the proudest father in all of Nova Scotia — here, let me replenish those glasses."

Mustache was suspicious. He stood looking down at Andy, frowning. "What's your full name, kid?"

"Andy Flynn."

"How old are you?"

"Eleven."

"And Vinny is your father?"

"That's right."

Glasses said doubtfully, "A kid's a serious responsibility, Vinny."

"Don't I know it. Now that I have Andy," said Vincent Flynn, "now he's no longer with his mother — may the angels and saints protect her and the Mother of Divine Sorrows give the soul of the poor unfortunate woman rest — my life has taken on a new purpose. You're right. It'll not be easy to raise a young boy, poor as I am, and with all the crime and wickedness there is in this city. It's a good thing we have the priests and the police to keep us all on the narrow path of virtue — have another drop; it'll warm yiz on a cold mornin'." He poured an inch and a half of whiskey into the policemen's glasses.

Mustache said, "I've two of my own, and I know what you mean. I worry about them. It's a different world they're born into nowadays, right enough. Jack here has three." He jerked his chin at Glasses. "Isn't that right, Jack?"

Jack looked into his empty glass and nodded sadly.

"Have a drop more before yiz go," said Andy's father, wielding the bottle. "It's dreadful cold out there."

"It's brutal," agreed Mustache, holding out his empty glass.

"Desperate," said Jack, doing the same.

"Stay out of trouble, Vinny," Mustache said before they left.

"And mind you take good care of the boy," said Jack, scowling.

Vinny jumped up and slipped the bolt back on the door, then opened the window and wrestled the boxes back inside, damp now with the rain.

Andy watched him. The boxes had cigarette brand names printed on them. "You didn't steal the cigarettes from a warehouse, did you, Dad?"

"Of course not! Those two thicks are paid to be suspicious; it's their job; but I don't hold it against them. All they want is the drink. They know very well I came by the cigs honestly. I don't have a vendor's license to sell cigarettes; that's my only crime."

"Then why not get a vendor's license?" asked Andy. "Then they can't put you in prison."

His father ripped open one of the boxes and started removing cartons of cigarettes and carrying them into the bedroom. Andy slid off the sofa and followed him in. He was on his knees pushing the cartons under the bed. "The license is dreadful expensive," his father explained. "Besides, I don't have a shop. City Hall will give no licenses to itinerant peddlers."

Andy didn't know what an itinerant peddler was. In fact, he found the whole cigarette business extremely

confusing. He knew in his heart that his father was innocent of any crime. But why had he lied about being home
all night? And why was he hiding the cigarettes from the
police, first outside on the fire escape and now under the
bed? Just because he had no license? And wasn't it a coin-
cidence that the warehouse was broken into the same
night his father came home with the boxes? And that his
father and Cassidy were seen at the warehouse?

Before any further disloyal suspicions could enter his
head, he said quickly, "Don't worry, Vinny, I won't let them
take you away to prison. I'll tell the judge what a good
father you are and how much I need you to look after me.
And even if they do put you behind bars, I'll rescue you in
a daring prison escape." Now he was calling him Vinny
instead of Father — what had happened to that new Dad
word he'd been practicing? — as if his father were a Mafia
hood or something.

"That's my boy!" Vinny grabbed him and kissed him
enthusiastically on the top of his tangled head. "The
finest son a man could have. Lucky, lucky man that I
am!"

His father *was* a Vinny, Andy realized; the name sat on
him like a tailored suit; he looked like a Vinny, he smelled
like a Vinny, he was the very essence of Vinnyness, which
meant he was dangerous and unpredictable and exciting; it
was as though he'd walked straight out of a Robert De Niro
movie. He was a man who took chances, who lived dangerously, who had the police searching his home, not like
boring old Clay, who had gone to his office every day in a

suit, shirt, and tie and whose only brushes with the law involved parking tickets.

Living dangerously. The words sent a thrill through him.

Vinny finished stashing the cartons of cigarettes under the bed; then he pulled on a pair of socks, an unironed shirt, and his food-stained sweater, and filled the inside pockets of his raincoat with packages of cigarettes torn fresh from their cartons, stuffing them into the deep secret pockets. Grabbing the empty raisins saucer off the table, he hurried into the kitchen. Andy heard the fridge door open and close. "What happened to the raisins I had in the fridge?" his father asked in alarm.

"I was hungry, so I ate them."

"Ah! They're not for eating, Andy. They're — now what will I do? — be a good boy and don't eat the raisins, you hear? I'll get more while I'm out." He went back to the fridge and placed the raisins saucer, now filled with milk, back in the center of the table, frowning and muttering to himself, "The milk will have to hold them." He grasped the bottom of the window, slid it up, and climbed out onto the wet fire escape.

"Hey! Where are you going?"

Vinny popped his head back inside and grinned. "Business."

"Why are you going out that way?"

"Fresh air. See you later, darlin'."

"You haven't washed, Vinny," Andy called after him. "Or cleaned your teeth. Or shaved. And you haven't had your cup of tea." But he'd had plenty of whiskey, he remembered. He leaned out the window and watched his father worriedly as he diminished in size, climbing down the iron steps. Andy hadn't washed either, and in all the excitement had forgotten to tell Vinny about the cockroaches. He slipped into his sneakers, grabbed his jacket, climbed out the window into the rain, and clanged his way down the rickety metal fire escape, hands sliding down rusted metal handrails while loose anchor bolts shifted and groaned in the crumbling concrete and the ancient structure shuddered and shifted with his weight as he hurried after Vinny. After his father. After Dad.

They scrambled down the fire escape after the boy.

" 'Twas dreadful cold out here," complained a Young One who had been trapped in a box of cigarette cartons on the fire escape when Vinny closed the window.

"Serves you right for sleeping in boxes," said another.

"Boxes are warm."

"Boxes get moved."

"It was I who closed the curtain so the police couldn't see — " began another proudly.

"Yes, well done," the Old One interrupted impatiently. "Now hurry! Keep your eyes on the boy."

9

HE SPOTTED HIM hurrying out of Noonan's. "Wait up, Vinny!" he yelled.

But his father didn't hear him, scuttling along, elbows flapping like the wings of a bird.

The thin rain was cold on Andy's face. As he hurried along behind Vinny, he noticed for the first time that his father had, not a limp exactly, but a slight dip, or tilt, on his right side, as if one leg was a bit shorter than the other. Vinny tilted.

The street was busy with pedestrians and traffic. Andy had to dodge around people. He ran and caught his father waiting at a corner for the light. "Wait, Vinny. I've got to talk to you."

Vinny smiled. "There's altogether too much talk in the world already, Andy. It's what causes most of the trouble." He looked left and right.

"I want to talk about … about …" Andy was confused. It was Vinny's business that puzzled him: stale cigarettes. "What will happen if they don't believe you didn't steal the cigarettes and they send you to jail? Or they arrest you for selling without a license? Don't you care?" Vinny walked fast. Andy almost had to run to keep up with him. "Stop and talk to me, Vinny."

Vinny turned sharply and disappeared into a pub called Ryan's.

Andy started to follow, but the stale smell of beer and smoke drove him back; he waited outside in the shelter of the doorway and watched people go by, leaning into the rain with their umbrellas.

Vinny came back to get him. "Come in for a minute, will you? I want you to meet some friends. Come in."

He followed him in reluctantly.

"This is my Andy," Vinny announced proudly to the men in the bar. "Aren't I the most fortunate man in all the world?"

The men crowded around enthusiastically and shook Andy by the hand or mussed his already mussed hair. Then they slapped Vinny on the back. "Sit down, Vinny, and I'll buy you a drink," said one of the men. "And the lad, too."

"I'll wait outside," said Andy, the smoke stinging his eyes.

When Vinny reappeared some minutes later, he set off again, his raincoat a little lighter, its tail flapping behind him like a parachute. "Go back," he said to Andy. "You'll be drowned following about after me."

"No. You've got to talk to me."

Vinny disappeared into another pub.

Andy waited.

Vinny popped his head back out the door. "Come in for a minute. Bob MacIntosh and Ian Holt are dying to meet you."

"No thanks. I'll wait here," said Andy.

Vinny went in and brought out a crowd to meet him. Andy had to shake hands with every one of them.

When Vinny emerged, they set off again.

"MacIntosh and Holt are Scots. But they're all right."

They were passing a coffee shop. Andy grabbed Vinny's arm and dragged him inside. "Let's sit and have a bottle of pop, Father, please? I need to talk to you, and I can't talk while I'm running to keep up."

Andy sat while Vinny shuffled reluctantly to the self-serve counter, returned with a tray laden with pop, glass, teapot, spoon, milk, and cup and saucer, and sat down opposite him and began stirring the pot with the spoon.

"Tell me things."

"What things?" Vinny lit a cigarette. His eyes smiled at Andy through curls of blue smoke.

"I need you to tell me things like … what will we do if they send you to jail?"

"That will never happen, Andy, rest your mind on that. Your father is completely innocent."

"I know. I believe you. But — "

"Don't worry your young head, Andy. Everything will be all right. There. Now do you feel better?"

Andy didn't feel better. He stared into his father's twinkling eyes. "I'll feel better when you stop selling cigarettes without a license and get a normal job. And I'll feel better when we find a nicer place to live." There, he'd said it: the Mayo was a dump.

His father looked hurt. "So you don't like my place."

"It's — well …" Andy faltered. Then he remembered the cockroaches. "There's cockroaches, thousands of them, swarming all over. You didn't warn me. What happens if they bite me and give me some disease? They give me the creeps. And the place is small with the two of us living there — I know you weren't expecting me, but you've had time by now to think about me, haven't you?" He searched Vinny's face. "Haven't you, Father?"

"Aren't you on my mind all the time? We'll make plans, Andy, I promise, okay?"

"And I get worried when you stay out late. I'm only eleven, you know. I'm a kid, not a grownup."

"You're more grownup than a lot of grownups I know. Anyway, leave it to me. I told you. We'll make plans, all right?" Vinny got up. "I'll be back in a jiff."

Andy looked around for him a few minutes later and saw him joking with customers up at the bar as he sold them cigarettes.

When he came back, Andy said, "What about the cockroaches?"

"Cockroaches will do you no harm, Andy. They don't bite. Take no notice of them. It's people you need to watch out for, not God's harmless creatures who were on this earth a million years before mankind and who'll be here a million years after the last one of us is gone."

Andy stayed glued to him for the rest of his rounds, asking questions about his cigarette business and making suggestions, trying to clear the confusion in his mind about having a father who was funny and daring and brave, a father liked by everyone, but who made a living selling stale cigarettes without a license. "I've got an idea!" he said. "You could open a little shop to sell the cigarettes! Then you'd get a license from City Hall. Or if you find a job, then I can help at home, I really can. I can wash dishes and fix things. Simple stuff. We can get a cookbook and I'll learn how to cook so supper's ready when you get home from work, and we'll get a dog to watch things while we're out. I know how to train dogs. It'll be great, you'll see."

Throughout this long speech and other speeches just like it, Vinny smiled happily and proudly at Andy, nodding his head in agreement at everything he said, speaking only to encourage him: "You're the great talker, Andy, I can see that all right. The great little talker. And you've the splendid wee head on your shoulders."

They bought a toothbrush and toothpaste — Andy didn't like the powder stuff in the packet — and a few other things at a corner store, including a bag of raisins.

"What's with the raisins?"

"Didn't you finish the last of them?"

Vinny sold his last package of cigarettes in a pub called The Pink Elephant. As he came out the door, Andy said, "So if you don't start your own little shop, will you give it up, the stale cigarette business?"

"I will, I will."

"You'll give it up?"

"Didn't I say I would? You'd convince the Divil himself."

"You promise?"

"I promise."

"And you'll find a job?" By now the rain had got through to his shirt.

"Ah, that'll be the difficult part, right enough."

"You'll find one, I know you will." Andy punched his father's arm encouragingly as they headed home through the rain.

Vinny stopped and they stood for a while watching the Mayo Rooms from the opposite side of the street.

"What are we waiting for?" asked Andy.

"Just making sure the coast is clear."

"The police, you mean?"

"Hmmn."

"What if they're inside, Father, waiting for you?"

He shook his head. "Not likely."

"Maybe I should go first and make sure it's safe."

"There's no necessity, Andy, I can tell how it is just by sniffing the air." He raised his head and sniffed. "It's all clear. Come on."

"Couldn't you stay with one of your pals until the heat is off?" A part of Andy was quite astounded to hear himself talking like a crime movie. His father was having a peculiar effect on him.

They entered by the front door. The place was quiet. No police. They climbed the stairs and stood outside the door listening. Nothing. They went inside. It was cold. The window was still open and rain had blown in, wetting the stained curtains and the scarred linoleum floor. Vinny closed the window and then disappeared into the bedroom. Andy followed him in. Vinny was on his knees pulling cigarette cartons out from under the bed and stacking them on the mattress.

"The police might come back and find them," said Andy. "Couldn't we dump them in somebody's garbage bin? You're not going to sell them anymore, you promised, remember?"

"Don't worry. Leave it to me." Vinny counted the cigarette cartons, then went into the kitchen, and Andy could hear him filling the kettle. Vinny called out to him, "I'll take good care of you, Andy, you'll see."

"You're the one who needs taking care of," Andy muttered to himself.

"Take off your wet things while I make us a cup of tea," Vinny shouted from the kitchen, "and help yourself to a dry shirt of mine in the bedroom."

Andy did as he was told. His father's shirt was too big, but not by so very much. Andy was hungry. "I'm hungry," he told Vinny as he came in with the cups and teapot.

"Hungry?" Vinny looked surprised.

"Starving."

"Wait. I'll be right back."

He was away only ten minutes, and brought back with him a box of sugared doughnuts, a dozen, assorted.

"Great," said Andy when he saw them. "I love doughnuts."

That evening Vinny stayed home with a newspaper called *The Sporting Life*, which he appeared to be reading without any of the problems he'd mentioned earlier about failing kindergarten, and even though the print was very tiny and the light was bad from the small bulb hanging shadeless from the center of the room. The back page of the newspaper had a picture of a horse race.

Vinny soon became restless and fidgety, smoking one cigarette after another and constantly jumping up to make tea, strengthened with a drop or two of whiskey. Except for the swish of traffic, the occasional diesel roar of a bus in the main street, and the tattoo of rain on the fire escape, the place was quiet.

There was nothing much for Andy to do in this bare room; there were no books, comics, or magazines, and the light was a bit dim for reading anyway. Andy lay back on the sofa, bored. "A TV would be nice," he said. "Or a CD player, or a radio so we could listen to music. Don't you like music, Father?"

Vinny didn't seem to be listening.

"My friends in Vancouver are probably surfing the Internet and listening to music. Or watching a video. Why's there no phone?"

"It's ten o'clock," said his father, peering at his wristwatch. "What time do eleven-year-olds go to bed in Vancouver?"

"I'm in Halifax now," he reminded his father, "which means I come under Halifax rules. What time do kids of eleven go to bed here?"

"Hmmn. I'm not sure. I'd think they'd be well away by ten, don't you?"

Andy gathered his new toothbrush and toothpaste, and washed in the kitchen. Then he spread the blankets over the sofa and climbed under. "You could tell me a story if you like."

"I don't know any stories."

"You used to tell me stories of the Little People, don't you remember?"

"You're too old for stories, Andy. You'll soon be old enough to vote."

"No. I'm still a kid, Father. Tell me a story like when I was little."

Vinny sighed. "Just for a few minutes, then." He carried his chair over to the sofa and sat beside Andy with his tea and cigarette. "I don't know if I remember any of the old stories."

"That's okay. Anything will do. And would you mind not smoking while you tell it? Secondhand smoke is deadly, didn't you know that?"

The rain played a riff on the window.

Vinny stubbed out his cigarette. "D'you remember the story of Tir Na n'Og?"

"That's the place where the Little People come from. The place you get to on a white horse. I remember it." And Andy did. It was coming back to him. Actually, part of it had never gone away: he often dreamed of white horses galloping over the ocean waves. "But you can tell me again if you like."

"Tir Na n'Og is the land of youth and immortality."

"Immortality is when nobody ever gets old or dies, right?"

"That's it. They live forever and beyond. It's a place of great beauty, with trees and lakes and rivers to beat anything you ever saw. Those who know say Tir Na n'Og is in the back of beyond. Humans and gods and the Sheehogue live there, side by side, in peace and harmony, with no death or sickness or pain."

"Sheehogue is the proper name for the Little People."

"That's it. Or the Sidhe, the fallen angels from heaven who were not good enough to be saved but not bad enough to be lost."

"How do you get to Tir Na n'Og?"

"Ah! That's the difficult part. first there must be moonlight. Then you must find a thorn tree where there's a faery ring — "

"What does a faery ring look like?"

"A circle of shamrock, or stones, or mushrooms, or buttercups, or the grass growing a certain way so it looks like a ring. Sometimes the Sheehogue will cast a spell, or play a *pishogue*, or trick, and they'll build a ring of cowpats to fool you. Or they will grow a ring of clover, or spinach, which they can't abide. Anyway, if you stand in a proper faery ring on special days, in the moonlight — "

"What special days?"

"There's different opinions. But for sure there must be no letter *r* in the day or in the month."

"No *r*?" Andy thought for a while, counting on his fingers. "That means only four days and four months."

"That's the truth of it, all right."

"So let's say it's a Sunday evening in May and the moon is shining and you find a faery ring. What do you do then?"

"To find the gateway to Tir Na n'Og, you walk around the ring nine times widdershins — that's anticlockwise — and you will see the gate open in front of you. Walk through the gate, and if the Sheehogue like you, they will put you up on a white horse and off you will gallop to the land of youth."

"And if they don't like you?"

"They will conjure a pishogue. You might walk through the gateway and tumble down a steep bank head over heels, for instance, and when you get up, the gateway and the faery ring have disappeared."

"Tir Na n'Og sounds like a hard place to find."

His father nodded. "It is. The back of beyond could be anywhere: deep under the ground or the ocean. The Sheehogue never tell. On top of all that, they like to enchant us with their pishogues. They can be cruel, too. Did you ever feel sharp pains or twinges in your side or your knee or some other place, and you don't know how they got there or where they came from?"

"Mother said they were growing pains."

"She was wrong, God rest her. It's the Sheehogue up to their pishogues, shooting their darts into you. They like to see the commotion on your face. And it's often the Sheehogue who cause the papers and leaves to swirl along the street and the dust to blow in your eyes. You turn your head sharp-like when you glimpse a bright color, or you close your eyes against a sudden burst of sunlight, and you walk smack into a heap of doggy do. Ha! It's the Sheehogue having their fun! And the louder you swear at them, the more they laugh at you. Sometimes, if there's no wind, and it's quiet enough, you might hear a faint tinkling sound, like tiny bells; that's the sound of the Sheehogue laughing."

Andy smiled. He was warm and drowsy. Tiny bells. His father's voice. He was four years old again. "More," he murmured. "Tell me more."

A heavy truck splashed by in the street.

"The Sheehogue are almost impossible to see. They don't make things easy for us, except sometimes, at a certain time of year, when the moonlight is shining on the thorn trees, anyone passing by with two good eyes in his head can see the Little People playing and dancing, and the faery music can be heard for a mile around. But men and women know to turn their heads away from the thorn trees because if they see the Sheehogue, then it's the terrible bad luck will come to them, sure as grass is green and thorn berry is red."

"Have you ... ever seen them, Father?"

"I have. Once. When I was a child like yourself."

"And did you turn your eyes away?"

"I did not. Children are exempt. If your heart's a child's heart, and if your eyes are clean, then you need never fear the moonlight or the thorn trees; you can look at them all you want and the Sheehogue will wave to you and bless you as you pass by and call your name."

"Will ... they know ... I changed my name ... to Andy?"

"They will know," whispered his father.

"I love the old stories," a Young One said wistfully. "Do you think he might tell the story of how Oisín fell in love with Niamh? It's the most beautiful story I ever — "

"You can ask Niamh herself when you get home," said her friend sarcastically.

"It's not the same. The boy's father is a fine story-teller. He is tender and true. Besides, Niamh exaggerates. If I asked anyone, it'd be Oisín."

"Shush, you two," whispered the Old One. "The boy sleeps."

10

IN SPITE OF HIS PROMISE and his good intentions, Vinny continued with his "business" until all the cigarettes were gone. "I meant that I'd stop as soon as the present supply ran out," he explained to Andy. "I couldn't leave them about the place. There will be no more after this, I promise."

In the days that followed, Andy felt stronger and, most important of all, was happy to be with his dad, who would soon get a proper job, and then their lives would be normal; it was simply a matter of time. When he inspected himself in the bathroom mirror, though it was covered in mildew and the light was small and dim, he saw that the bruises were just about gone from his face. His eyes seemed brighter. But his dark hair, unbrushed and uncombed, was longer and wilder. He didn't look too clean. In Vancouver they'd had three bathrooms with plenty of hot water and shampoo and hair conditioner and body lotion and he could shower whenever he wanted. But here ...

There was also the problem of his soiled socks and underwear. He had only the one set and needed extras badly. His mother and Clay were not here to nag him. Dad wouldn't nag him. Dad didn't even seem to care if he went to school. Dad was great.

But it would be useful to own an extra pair of underpants.

They were going out, closing the door behind them, when Vinny remembered something and went back into the room. He grabbed the saucer that sat permanently in the center of the table and poured into it a teaspoonful of raisins from the new packet.

"Why are you doing that?"

"Because it's the first place they look."

"Who?"

"The Sheehogue, of course. They love raisins. It's their favorite food."

Andy remembered. How could he have forgotten? His father left food for the Little People. "So they will leave us alone and not pester us with their pishogues," Vinny explained, surprised that any explanation was needed.

Vinny usually forgot to give him pocket money unless he asked for it, a few dollars at a time. Vinny was on welfare, but most of his money, Andy guessed, came from the stale cigarettes. "You can't take care of me from a prison cell, *Father*," Andy reminded him, in case he had forgotten his promise to find a job.

The end of the second week seemed to come quickly. When Andy looked back on it, he realized how little he'd done. He had been rising late, about the same time as Vinny, breakfasting on tea and a doughnut from the fridge — Vinny seldom ate them — and spending the afternoons, while Vinny was out looking for a job, in empty idleness, sitting out on the creaky fire escape if it wasn't raining, or wandering about the neighborhood, buying himself a chocolate bar if he was hungry. He saw a crowd of kids one afternoon playing, yelling, running in a nearby schoolyard and stood and watched them through the iron railing until the bell summoned them back inside.

He missed his friends in Vancouver.

And his feet itched to kick a soccer ball.

He got an extra key made for the apartment — his father had kept meaning to get it done but always forgot, so Andy took care of it himself.

One morning, just as Andy was leaving the apartment — Vinny hadn't come home the night before, so Andy hadn't slept much — two men, one big, the other small, in black trench coats, came up the stairs and stopped him in the hallway. The small man carried a notebook. The big man was very big and wore sunglasses.

"You're Vinny Flynn's kid, am I right?" asked the small man.

"Maybe I am and maybe I'm not. Who wants to know?"

The man, not much taller than himself, reminded Andy of a Chihuahua dog.

"Is Vinny in?"

"No, he's out."

"Didn't come out the front door," said the small man. "We been waitin'. You sure he's out?"

"Sure I'm sure."

The man checked his wristwatch and made a note in his book. "Do you know when he be back?"

"No idea. He's on tour. He coaches the Canadian soccer team."

"Funny," said the man. "Tell him Fingers Agostino dropped by. Tell him we be back."

The big man cracked his knuckles. Fingers nodded at the big man. They turned and swaggered to the stairs. Just as they started down, Fingers tripped, falling into his sidekick, and they both tumbled, cursing and swearing, down the stairs.

"You okay?" Andy called down after them, trying to keep his face straight.

So that was why Vinny used the fire escape: not only the police but the Halifax Mafia were after him. Something else to worry about: those men looked mean.

His father came home just after midnight smelling of the pub. He had been away twenty-eight hours. Andy said nothing about spending a sleepless night of worry and waiting. When he told him about the two men, Vinny shrugged, unconcerned.

"He said to tell you his name, Fingers Agostino."

"Don't bother your head about Fingers Agostino. He used to be a pickpocket. But now he likes to terrorize good, lawful, hardworking folk like your poor father, but we

Flynns are not so easily intimidated, are we, Andy?" He laughed.

The next afternoon, while Vinny searched for work, Andy was bored with nothing to do. He went out, locking the door behind him, and walked around the shops in the downtown, looking into the faces of the women, hoping to see his mother. He thought he saw her once, in a crowd — something about the tilt of her head and the way she walked — and hurried after her, but it turned out to be someone else, a much younger woman. After a couple of hours his feet were sore. It started to rain, so he dodged into a coffee shop. He helped himself to a mug of hot chocolate at the self-serve bar, and sat at a table near the door where he could keep watch for a break in the weather. The place became crowded with others sheltering from the rain. School was out. A crowd of kids came in. Two high school girls in ski jackets and jeans asked if they could share his table, and without waiting for an answer sat down and began talking and giggling together. They were drinking bottles of pop. One girl had brown hair and glasses, and the other girl's hair was a gingery red. Andy thought again of his friends in Vancouver. Having a best friend was important. He really missed Ben. After a while, the girl with the brown hair turned to Andy and said, "You don't go to St. Dominic's, do you?"

Andy shook his head.

She looked him over. "You're a street kid, right?"

Andy didn't understand what she meant, so said nothing.

The two girls stared at him with distaste, sneers on their faces, and then moved their chairs, turning away from him to resume their giggling chatter.

The door of the coffee shop suddenly blew open and a powerful wind toppled coffee cups and whirled napkins into the air. The two girls at Andy's table screamed as their pop exploded out of the bottles and hosed their clothes while, at the same time, the wind tangled their hair and blew their unzipped ski jackets so they flapped wildly. They danced and screamed in terrified confusion, pulling futilely at their jackets. Then, as suddenly as it had come, the wind ceased.

Andy made his way home. The rain had stopped. He had never experienced anything quite like that coffee shop wind before. Halifax weather was certainly quite unpredictably different.

Vinny came home late, smelling of the pub as usual. Andy had stayed awake, waiting for him.

"You find a job, Dad?"

His father sighed. "There isn't one job to be had in the length and breadth of Nova Scotia." He threw himself into the easy chair. "You should be in bed, my lad."

"I was just going." Andy wanted to talk. Alone all day, he had felt cut off; he needed to talk — about anything, it didn't matter what so long as he didn't feel so cut off. "How come the raisins are still always there when we get home?" he asked. "I thought you said raisins are their favorite."

His father swiveled his head and glanced at the saucer. "What you see, Andy, is not the same raisins, not at all."

"What's different about them?"

His father stood. "The Sheehogue have taken what they need, which is the heart or the essence of the raisins. Raisin-ness is all they require, what you might call the life force of the fruit. What they leave wouldn't nourish a fly." He started for his room. "In fact, if you were to eat them you could sicken and die."

"Maybe we should leave some on the floor for the cockroaches," Andy called after him as the bedroom door closed.

"Those men. The ones in the black coats. Did they fall or were they pushed?" asked the Old One.

"What do you think?" giggled a Young One.

"It is not proper to cause hurt unless they wished harm on the boy," the Old One reminded them patiently.

"We could not admire their attitude," said one of the others. "Nor did we enjoy those mean schoolgirls. As you sow, so shall you reap."

"You get what's coming to you," a Very Young One growled, translating the ancient tongue into American-accented English.

"Which in your case," said the Old One, "is the first watch. Wake me if anything occurs."

11

THE THIRD WEEK PASSED without Vinny finding a job. He stayed out all night again, and got home at noon the next day, bleary-eyed and stinking of cigarettes and liquor. Then he slept till evening and went out again. Andy worried about him.

On the Monday afternoon of the fourth week, Andy looked out the window to see a pale sun emerge from gray clouds and shimmer brightly in the pothole puddles. Vinny got up, rubbing the sleep from his eyes, and made for the kitchen. Andy heard the clink of a bottle. Then his father returned to his room and dressed.

Andy, now sick and tired of so much freedom every day, and mindful of the two girls in the coffee shop — the looks of disgust on their faces — told his father that he was ready to go shopping for clothes. He was starting to smell. And he was cold most of the time. It seemed bizarre to be telling his father, an adult, what needed to be done, but in some ways, Andy was beginning to realize, Vinny was like a child. Andy would have to be the one to get things started.

"I need a warm jacket," he told Vinny. "And some socks and shirts and underclothes, that's all. And my own towel. And you need clothes, too, Vinny."

"Don't I wish I could, but I can't go with you, Andy. I've too much to do. If I give you the money, could you go on your own, d'you think?" He took out a handful of crumpled bills from his pocket.

"No, Vinny, I won't go on my own. You're coming with me whether you like it or not. So get ready and let's go. If you don't, then I'll walk through Dan Noonan's naked and I'll tell everyone you're not taking proper care of me."

Vinny laughed. "You've the great spirit, Andy, so you have. But you're right. I'm no kind of father to you at all. Naked in Noonan's! Ha! Wouldn't that give them something to talk about!" He threw his arms about Andy enthusiastically and whiskey-stubble-kissed his cheek. "Give me a few minutes to throw something on and we'll go together. We'll get the things you need and then we'll have something to drink down on the waterfront, how would that be?"

Vinny shaved. Andy knew his habits by now: he shaved only once a week, if that, and had to be reminded sometimes to brush his teeth.

They shopped in Eaton's children's department for a warm winter jacket. Andy had been wearing the thin nylon jacket ever since he left the hospital in Vancouver. The new one was a green-and-black parka that came down warmly over his thighs. Vinny's stock of coins and crumpled bills — he didn't seem to use a wallet — grew smaller as he let Andy pick out whatever else he needed, socks and pants and T-shirts and a pair of comfortable walking boots. Andy said, "I could use an extra blanket, too. A thick one. I get cold at night."

Vinny carried the new blanket in a bag; Andy wore his new jacket and boots, carrying his other new things in a shopping bag.

"Now it's your turn; let's get you some new cords and a sweater," said Andy.

"Ah! Not today, Andy darlin'. It's getting late. We'll come another time when I'm more in the mood to try things on."

The waterfront cafés were crowded, but they found a warm and sheltered spot outside on the deck with a view of the boats in the marina. Vinny ordered a pint of beer for himself, with a whiskey chaser, and a hamburger and pop for Andy.

"Dad, please? Couldn't we move to a nicer place?" asked Andy while they waited for their order.

His father looked worried.

"Nicer than the Mayo Rooms. Vin — Dad, face it, it's a dump. It's not only the cockroaches, but the building is old and dirty and it's freezing cold, and there's no proper bathroom — "

"The Mayo is fine, Andy, just fine." Vinny was unusually firm. "We can get something for the cockroaches if they bother you, but rents are terrible high all over. We can't afford to be throwing money down the drain, paying high rent in some fancy condohoonium when all we need is a place to boil a kettle and rest our heads for a few hours."

"We need more than a place to sleep, Vinny! I want us to live in a proper home, not a roach-infested garbage dump with no heat and no bathroom of our own!"

"A home?" Vinny scratched his head, as if the idea were new to him. "We will make it a proper home, Andy. But these things just take time. Have a little patience."

Their order came. *"Sláinte!"* Vinny took a swig of beer from the heavy glass.

"Sláinte," Andy replied, raising his bottle of pop and drinking. He poured salt and ketchup on his fries. The burger was a fat one, with lettuce and onions. His mouth watered at the sight of it. He couldn't remember when he'd last had a burger.

He could see that Vinny wasn't about to budge on the idea of a new place, so he said, "You promise to do something about the cockroaches?"

"As soon as I get a chance I'll have the little divils marching out the door, and down to the harbor like the Pied Piper's rats throwing themselves into the river Weser."

"And get an electric heater?"

"Hmmn. I'd have to sneak it in. If Rooney found out, he'd put up the rent."

"So you'll get one?"

He looked gloomy, like a kid losing his comics. "I suppose it could be done."

Andy grinned. "Okay. If we can't move to a nicer place,

but you get a heater and do something about the cock-roaches, then I guess we could manage with the Mayo a lit-tle while longer. Could we put up a partition on one side of the sofa as well, the kind you see in offices? Where every-one's in a separate cubicle? It'd be like having my own room. Then all I'd need is some small cardboard boxes I could stack against the wall to keep my things in, or a lit-tle chest of drawers, a secondhand one would do, and — hey, we forgot to buy me a towel."

Vinny started to say something, but Andy rushed on, the words leapfrogging out of his mouth.

"I've got a few ideas how we can change things, too, make the place a bit nicer, a cover for the sofa and chair and a few cushions, like Mom used to do, and we could paint the walls, and — "

"Hold on there," interrupted Vinny. He looked worried again.

Andy waited for him to go on, but he seemed lost for words.

Finally Vinny said, "It sounds brilliant, right enough." He nodded gravely as though these were all weighty mat-ters requiring serious thought and consideration, then, as though taking medicine, he tossed back his whiskey in one swallow.

"There's just one more thing I'd like."

"What's that?"

"Something important."

"Go on."

"*Really* important."

"Spit it out, why don't you!"

Andy hesitated. "Well, I'm on my own quite a lot." He paused. "I need ... I'd like a dog." Before his father could say anything, Andy rushed on: "I've always wanted a dog, a pup I could bring up and train, but I've never had one. Mom used to say I was too young to know how to look after a dog. Clay didn't want one in the house either. But I'm old enough now, don't you think? I know how to take care of a dog and feed him and train him to obey signals and he wouldn't be any trouble and ..." He stopped. His father stared and blinked as if he didn't know what a dog was, as if it were some alien creature he never knew existed. "Not a big dog," Andy reassured him, "just a medium-sized dog, and he wouldn't have to be anything special, like ..." He stopped again.

Silence.

"Father?"

"A dog," said Vinny.

"For me to keep and look after, to be my friend."

Vinny seemed to shake himself out of his stupor. "A dog! Well, why didn't you say? A dog is it? Every boy should have a dog. We'll have to look into it. Leave it to me."

"When, Dad? When do you think I could get a dog? We could go together to the pound — that's where they keep stray animals — and pick one out. You could help me."

"We will do just that, we'll go to the pound and pick one out. We will interview every dog they have in the place and inspect their little paws and teeth. We will pick the very best dog we can find. Let's talk about it again next week, all right? I'll be terrible busy for the next few days trying to find a job."

Andy saw very little of Vinny over the next few days; he left the apartment each afternoon, often by way of the fire escape, preoccupied, though never forgetting to leave a few fresh raisins on the table, his mind bent on finding a job. Andy reminded him of the heater and the poison for the cockroaches. Vinny said he was working on them. What about the dog? Could they go soon to the pound? Maybe it would be better to wait until he found a job first, Vinny said, before taking on added responsibilities.

Andy watched out the window one evening, waiting for his father to come home. It was raining. He had promised to be back by six with something for supper, and now it was seven. At seven-fifteen he heard the loud *kerthunk-kerthunk* of an old engine; he went to the window and peered down through the fire escape at a battered old truck at the curb, and he saw his father climb out, followed by the driver, Cassidy. They each carried a cardboard box, supported on their stomachs, up the steps of the side entrance and inside the building.

Andy opened the door and stood waiting for them.

His father was the first to appear. "Howyeh, Andy?" he said, smiling at him as he passed through, smelling of smoke and beer, into the living room with the box. The box said *Jameson's Irish Whiskey* on its sides. Cassidy's box was identical. "Howyeh, Andy?" he said as he lowered the box from his big belly to the floor and turned immediately for the door. "See you later, Vinny," he said, and he was gone.

Andy looked at the boxes. Twelve bottles in each box. Stale whiskey. He didn't want to know where it had come from. "Did you find a job?"

"Ah, Andy, there's no jobs. It's no use looking." He shook his head at the hopelessness of it all, then broke into mournful song. "She's the most distressful country that ever yet was seen, for they're hangin' men and women for the wearin' o' the green."

"You can go hang, too, for all I care!" Andy cried. Vinny hadn't even looked for a job. Andy suddenly knew this without being told, and he could do nothing to stop the swell of anger that rose in his chest. "You didn't even look for a job, Vinny!" he yelled, grabbing his new jacket and fleeing out the door, down the stairs, and out into the rain.

He didn't return until much later, and by then he was thoroughly soaked and thoroughly tired.

" 'Tis a terrible country for harsh rain!" complained a Young One as they all trooped in behind the boy.

"But Vancouver is dreadful wet," another Young One reminded her.

"Aye, but Vancouver rain is soft."

"Not as soft as Irish rain."

"Aye, Irish is softest, right enough."

They struggled out of their wet things, hung them on the yellow nylon rope to dry, and then sat shivering on the windowsill, damp and dispirited, drying one another off with the grubby curtain.

"I want to go home to the meadow," the Very Young One cried.

"There, there," crooned the Old One, patting her slim shoulders. "It won't be long now. We're already halfway to our goal. Duty is a stern master. Soon we will be done. Have patience, my dear."

12

HIS FATHER WAS UP by eleven o'clock the next morning. Andy heard the clink of bottle on glass from the kitchen before his father gave his face a cat lick with water and towel. He didn't shave. Then he loaded four bottles of whiskey into his raincoat pockets, two on each side like saddlebags, straining the tired fabric to its limit. A further four went into a shopping bag. "They were a gift," he explained to Andy, smiling through several days' ginger stubble. "I'll sell them off and then we'll be done with them, and first thing Monday I'll look for a job, I promise."

Vinny's promises.

"I'll be off on my rounds, then." Vinny changed the raisins, then stepped out into the hall and stood still for a few seconds, like a deer, ears cocked, listening, nose sniffing the air for danger. He came back in, closed the door and climbed out the window, making his way carefully down the fire escape. "See you in a while, Andy," he called when he reached the bottom.

Andy watched him move away down the street, his tilt slightly more pronounced because of the saddlebags.

After his father had gone, Andy felt empty and unhappy. His head hurt. He lay on the sofa and fell asleep.

"Dad, would it be a good idea for you to start getting up earlier in the mornings? To find a job? The early bird ... you know?"

Vinny laughed. "Ah, I will, I will. I had a few words with a man who might have something coming up in the next week or two. Patience is a great thing."

"What about the heater? The weather's colder."

"Didn't I already talk to a man who knows electric fires. He's looking out for one for me."

"And the cockroaches?"

"Ah! Well, I spoke to a man who knows roaches and he's coming around soon. The night of the full moon is the proper time to catch them, he says."

"Are you sure? There's an r in the month, don't forget. Aren't cockroaches safe in r months?"

"It must be my influence; you're turning out to be such a clever, witty child, Andy." Vinny stroked his hair fondly and kissed his cheek. "But we'll solve all our problems, never you fear."

On the occasional evenings that Vinny stayed home, he sometimes answered coded — two slow, pause, two fast — knocks on the door. He invited nobody in, but talked or whispered for a few seconds with each caller before sending them on their way with a small slip of paper for the betting shop, or with a bottle of whiskey.

Tonight had been particularly busy, with knocks at regular intervals throughout the evening. At ten o'clock Vinny said, "Bedtime, Andy."

"Tell me a story."

"For a few minutes, then." When Andy was under his new blanket, Vinny sat on the edge of the sofa.

"There's a big old library downtown," said Andy. "I'm going to join and have something to read in the evenings, seeing as how we've got no TV or radio or anything. Do you think we could get a reading lamp?"

"Good idea, Andy, we'll have a reading lamp. You're lighting up my life, so you are."

"Tell me a Tir Na n'Og story."

"Very well. I'll tell you what happened to young Lord Fitzgerald when he swore to love an orphan girl, swore to love her forever and beyond. Are you ready?"

"I'm ready."

"The Little People were singing and dancing under the hawthorn tree one bright moonlit — "

"Why does it always have to be moonlight? What's so important about moonlight?"

"Food for the soul. The Little People need to charge their spiritual batteries, same as us, which is why we pray and go to church. Now can I go on?"

"I thought you said they need raisins."

"They do indeed. Raisins are food for the body. Body and soul is the whole man. If you keep interrupting — "

"I won't interrupt anymore. Go on."

"One bright moonlit night when Lord Fitzgerald was very young, he heard the sounds of the Sheehogue singing and dancing in the meadow ..."

"I love the story of Lord Fitzgerald and the orphan girl."

"Ah, don't we all?"

"Will ye hush and let us listen?"

13

ANDY WOKE IN THE NIGHT with the feeling there was someone in the room. He held his breath, listening. Scratching sounds coming from ... where? Heart racing, he sat up and looked around quickly. The anti-cockroach light was still on and there was nobody in the room. Vinny's door was open, which meant he wasn't yet home. Andy listened. There it was again: *scratch-scratch*. He looked around. Nothing. Then *scratch-scratch* again; from the kitchen. He slid off the sofa, blanket about his shoulders, and tiptoed to the kitchen. An enormous gray rat had been sniffing something on the floor; when it saw Andy, it scurried away and disappeared behind the stove.

Another good reason for keeping a dog.

He couldn't sleep after that, wishing Vinny would come home, listening for the rat, his mind a kaleidoscope of colliding images and sounds: bet you never thought I'd end up in cold Halifax place of my birth living with Vinny and rats and cockroaches huh Mother where are you now and Clay do you still see Clay and can you see me here Mother with

Vinny my father your husband once and a dirty great rat in the kitchen, can you?

Vinny was up early the next morning, by ten o'clock, early for him. Andy hadn't heard him come in.

"There was a rat last night," was the first thing Andy said to him. "In the kitchen."

"A rat was it? Are you sure it wasn't a happypotamus?"

"It's not funny! I don't like rats near my bed."

"There, there. I'll get a trap from Rooney and we'll be rid of him. Leave it to me."

"A dog would keep the place free of rats, especially a terrier. And he wouldn't cost much to feed."

"Terriers are lovely dogs. We had an Irish terrier one time I was working in Edenderry in the bog. He could run the legs off a hare, he was that quick. The rat was in the kitchen, you say? You should have called me." He kissed the top of Andy's head. "I'll not let the rats get you, Andy darlin'. You're safe with me." He gave Andy's shoulder a sympathetic squeeze. "What do you say I make us a nice cup of tea?"

Vinny disappeared into the kitchen, and from the glassy clinks Andy knew it wasn't only a nice cup of tea that Vinny was making for himself.

He woke another night, or early morning, to the sounds of a fight. It was on his floor, at the back of the building somewhere. A woman screamed and a door slammed. This was followed by a man shouting and swearing. Next came violent door-pounding and more screaming.

He was scared.

Luckily, Vinny was home. He got up and sat beside Andy and stroked his head and sang a soothing lullaby about a drowsy grandmother falling asleep at a spinning wheel. Andy closed his eyes and went back to sleep.

Five weeks.

For Andy, one dreary day was much like another. By now he was thoroughly fed up being alone with nothing to do. What a month ago had seemed glorious freedom was now gloomy captivity. So he asked his father one evening about school — he was never going to find any friends if he didn't go to school, he'd decided; looking through the wrong side of the iron railings wasn't good enough; he needed to play some soccer with a bunch of kids his own age.

"School is a grand idea," Vinny said. "I should have thought of it myself. I will pay a call at the education office tomorrow morning, first thing, and see about school for you."

But the next day came and went without anything being done.

Feeling desolate and lonely, dreading even one more day in dreary idleness, Andy resolved to find a school for himself. Friends and soccer were too important to leave to Vinny while he was busy looking for a job. Andy couldn't expect his father to find friends for him, too, so he picked out the school for himself, St. Dominic's, the one with the railings, a few blocks from the Mayo, an old gray building

111

that looked more like a fortress than a school. It was Catholic, which was fine. He was supposed to be Catholic anyway, though he and his mother hadn't gone to church much, especially after Clay entered their lives. He decided to enroll as a new student the next morning. If they asked him about his father, he would say Vinny was working and couldn't come, which wasn't exactly a lie.

In the afternoon he found his way to the dog pound and looked at the strays in their cages. There were only three dogs, two big miserable ones with runny eyes who showed no interest in him, and a smaller, lively one who jumped at the bars, barking with excitement.

The pound keeper was a self-important man, pale and plump, who wore a Hitler mustache and a black uniform and sat on a swivel chair in a tiny office reading the newspaper. Andy asked him if he could take the small brown dog with the floppy ears, but was told to return with his mother or father. The man didn't look up from his newspaper. "Can't hand an animal over to a juvenile, sorry."

"But he wants me to take him," said Andy. "See how excited he is."

"Sorry."

"Please," said Andy. "I'll take good care of him, I promise."

The man remained engrossed in his newspaper.

A wind started up and the swivel chair started spinning. The pound keeper yelled in fear as he clutched the arms of the chair. The chair toppled and threw him to the floor.

"I better go," said Andy, hurrying out the door. "I'll be back, Brownie," he yelled at the dog.

"I would have spun the creature into a black hole had you not stopped me," said a Young One angrily.

"We *Sidhe* strive to be like the meadow grass," instructed the Old One. "We bend with the force of the wind. You must learn patience."

"Is that why you do nothing to rid us of the great ugly rat in the kitchen?" jeered the Young One. "Or is it because you are afraid?"

The Old One smiled. "As well as patience, we must learn that all creatures are the same: each has the right to live its life."

14

"TODAY WE'RE HAVING BREAKFAST for a change," Andy declared the next morning. "I took some money from your coat pocket and bought stuff for pancakes, okay? And a jar of maple syrup."

Vinny still hadn't found a job, and the rat had appeared in the kitchen again last night. Andy hadn't mentioned it yet. Vinny had done nothing about the rat. He'd done nothing about the cockroaches either. Vinny sat drinking his nice cup of tea while Andy stirred his disappointments into the pancake batter.

"Breakfast is a grand idea," agreed Vinny.

"Do you ever go to church on Sundays?" Andy asked him from the hot plate.

"Huh? Church is it? I do, the odd time. Good Friday, Easter. And Christmas," he added.

"Which one? St. Dominic's?"

"That's the one."

"Could we start going to church, Father? Together, I mean, Sunday mornings? Mom used to take me sometimes when I was little. I liked it. Everyone was dressed in their best, and the girls and women had hats and gloves and rosary beads. We could take a prayer book and go early and always sit in the same pew and sing the hymns together. What do you say?" He poured batter into the hot pan.

"It would be grand altogether. Your mother could sing the hymns like a linnet when she was a girl. And at the ceilidh she'd sing 'Danny Boy' and have everyone crying."

"I'm starting school today," said Andy.

"School?" Vinny sounded surprised. "What school?"

"St. Dominic's. I can walk there in five minutes." Andy put a pancake down in front of him.

"They didn't ask to see me?"

"I haven't been there yet. I'll just go to the school office and enroll as a new kid from Vancouver. If they ask, I'll tell them you're at work."

"Just like that?"

"Just like that."

"This pancake looks lovely." Vinny picked up his fork. "Education is the wonderful thing. I never had much of it myself, but I'm glad to see you taking my advice. School is a remarkable idea."

Andy brought his own pancake, flipped a second pancake onto Vinny's plate, and sat opposite.

"I only want what's best for you, Andy."

"I know that, Vinny. That's why I went to the pound yesterday. I found a dog I like. One that will keep the rats away. Might be good for the cockroaches, too. And he'll be a great guard dog. He's only a pup; he's brown with floppy ears and big brown eyes. I called him Brownie and I could see his eyes light up; he liked his new name, I could tell. You'll love him, I know you will. But you have to come with me to sign the papers, okay? After I get home from school?"

"Andy, I've got to be straight with you. The dog will have to wait till I find a job, and that's all there is to it. Once I have a job, you will have all the time in the world to find a dog, I can't be straighter than that."

Disappointment, like a fist in his face. "You don't want me to have a dog. You're just like my mother and Clay." He knew he was whining but couldn't help himself.

"I promise you'll have a dog as soon as we're on our feet. Leave it to me."

The disappointment turned to anger. "You're always making promises! The problem with you, Vinny, is you always break them. A promise to you is just a way of putting things off! You just don't *ever* get things done."

Vinny said nothing, finishing only one of his pancakes, his face solemn.

Then, "You're the great little cook, Andy; that was lovely. And as far as getting things done … you're right." His voice grew quiet. "I'm not much good as a father, am I?" He stared miserably down at the uneaten pancake.

When Andy saw the distress on his father's face, his anger fled as quickly as it had come. "Considering you're only a learner …" Andy was about to make a joke of it, but

116

stopped himself when he saw his father's despairing face, the slump of his shoulders, the sadness in his eyes.

"To tell the truth, Andy, your father has never been much good at anything, and that's the size of it."

"You mustn't say that ..."

"No ... no, it's true. I'm no good to anyone and no good to myself."

Andy started to put his arms around his father, but Vinny got up and, without another word, went into his room and closed the door.

Andy stared at the door helplessly. Vinny had never done anything like this before; it was totally unusual. He cleaned up the breakfast things. The pancakes had been good, the first real breakfast he'd ever made, but his achievement was spoiled by the thought of having caused his father's sudden depression. It just wasn't like Vinny to be so unhappy; maybe looking for a job was getting him down. Andy threw himself onto the sofa and felt himself sinking into the swamp of his father's misery. He began to see failure and despair worn into the torn, grubby curtains, smeared on the stained walls, ground into the shoddy furniture. Vinny's life was a weight pressing Andy down further into the swamp; even the thought of being with kids his own age, in school, wasn't enough to cheer him up. He would leave the school enrollment idea till tomorrow; today he didn't feel so great.

It was only eleven o'clock in the morning, but he closed his eyes and fell asleep.

When he awoke, Vinny was sitting in his chair reading *The Sporting Life.* "It's late," he said, "but you were sleeping like a baby. I couldn't wake you up."

Whether it was because of Vinny's earlier sadness, or because of something else — an atmosphere of hopelessness that Vinny had created in the room, or the heavy gloom of the day, the rain beating on the fire escape outside — Andy had a sense of foreboding, a feeling that something bad was about to happen, a black premonition that clutched his heart.

Vinny, out of cigarettes, got up and went into his room. Andy could hear him ripping at a fresh carton — he never seemed to run out of them — as a knock came on the door, the usual code.

"Vinny," Andy called in to him, "it's one of your secret agents at the door."

Vinny opened the door and two men burst in, black trench coats, one man big, the other small. Andy recognized them: the Halifax Mafia — Fingers Agostino and his sidekick.

Vinny was fast: he turned and sprang to the window, throwing it wide open for an emergency escape, but couldn't climb out because the big man, just as fast, had a grip on his shirt and was pulling him back in. Andy ran into the kitchen, grabbed the frying pan, and jumped up, swinging it at the bodyguard's head, catching him on the back of the neck. The bodyguard swore, releasing Vinny, and swatted Andy like a fly, catching him in the chest and catapulting him back against the wall. Andy, the wind driven out of him, collapsed on the floor in a daze while Vinny escaped out the window.

"After him!" yelled Fingers.

The two men followed Vinny out the window, scrambling onto the fire escape.

Andy struggled to his feet and leaned out the window. He heard a screech of metal and saw part of the fire escape bend away from the wall as the combined weight of the three men caused anchors to rip from the crumbling wall and the structure to buckle under the strain. Someone screamed. Andy saw the two black trench coats flutter to the ground like swooping bats, and then he saw Vinny at the bottom of the fire escape hanging upside down, his head about fifteen feet above the ground, arms hanging loose as if he were dead.

"Vinny!" Andy yelled. He plunged forward, trying to climb out onto the fire escape, but something was holding him back. It felt like Fingers' sidekick dragging him back into the room, but that was impossible: the sidekick was lying dead, or unconscious, on the ground below. "Vinny!" Andy yelled again as he struggled to climb out the window but it was no good; he was held fast. He turned away from the window and was free and ran downstairs.

15

VINNY WASN'T DEAD. Andy had been quick getting down to the telephone in the manager's office. The police car, fire truck, and ambulance were not long getting to the Mayo.

Firemen climbed up and released Vinny's trapped foot from the twisted metal of the fire escape while Andy stood looking up at them.

Had he found his father after all these years only to lose him again? Vinny, he prayed, don't die on me!

Fingers and his friend were strapped to stretchers and loaded into the ambulance.

Vinny, his face bloody, was on the next stretcher. "Vinny!" yelled Andy. "Are you okay? Vinny! Speak to me!" But his father's eyes were closed.

"Is he dead?" Andy danced wildly around the medics.

"He's alive," said one.

"He'll be okay, kid," said the other. "Don't worry. Get in the ambulance."

Andy climbed into the ambulance with his father and then spent the next hour waiting anxiously in Emergency, praying still, watching the medical staff coming and going, walking the floor, sitting, walking the floor again. A nurse asked him questions and wrote down his answers.

When the nurse had gone, he sat biting lip and finger-nails. What if his father died and he was left alone? What would he do? There was nobody else, only Aunt Mona, and he didn't want to live with her. Where would he live?

Poor Vinny — was he in pain?

A doctor introduced himself. Dr. Julic. Andy's father would mend. Crutches for a week or two. Head sutures. Nothing too serious. What were sutures? Stitches, that was all. Poor Vinny, head stitched like a soccer ball. But he would be all right. Andy felt the relief surge in his chest.

"What about the other two men?"

Fingers and his sidekick had broken their legs.

It was almost two hours before Vinny appeared, dragging himself along on crutches like a wounded soldier, a nurse at his elbow helping and encouraging. The dressing cir-cling his head covered a gash to his temple. His foot, swollen to the size of a turnip, was heavily bandaged. Obviously in some pain, he smiled wearily when he saw Andy waiting for him.

The nurse offered to call a taxi, but Vinny said he could do it himself. The nurse left. "I'll be only a minute," he said to Andy.

Andy sat in the waiting room. He could see his father's back at the telephone in the hospital entrance. He seemed to be making not one but several calls.

The taxi took them home. Andy helped his father up the stairs and onto the sofa. His foot had to be kept raised, off the floor.

Andy made him tea.

"Throw in a drop of whiskey," said Vinny. "I need it to clear my poor head. Then leave the bottle here beside me."

Andy took the mug back to the kitchen, poured a little of the tea into the sink to make room for the whiskey, and topped up the mug from the whiskey bottle on the counter. Then he put the tea and the bottle on the floor beside the sofa where his father could reach them.

Vinny stirred his tea. He seemed depressed. Or was still in shock from his brush with death. "Thanks for your help, Andy. I don't know what I'd've done without you." He stared. "You look a bit flushed. Are you all right?"

"I'm fine," said Andy, but he didn't feel fine. His head felt like it was about to burst; cockroaches and scorpions crawled in his belly.

"I'll not be dancing for a while," said Vinny. "Wasn't that the madness? On the fire escape? I was fortunate not to break my neck. Upside down I was, my whole life turned upside down, Andy, can you believe that?"

Vinny drank his tea, then balanced himself on his crutches and limped to his room to sleep. Andy lay on the sofa to rest his pounding head and battle with his demons.

The next day Andy still had a headache, and the feeling of doom had not gone away.

122

He had felt it minutes before the fire escape accident and he felt it still.

It was like a vulture hovering over him.

Something waiting to happen. Waiting to tear out his liver.

Again, Vinny wasn't his usual happy self; he lay on the sofa, foot propped up on the arm, worried and depressed. Andy put it down to pain from the injuries.

Vinny groaned.

"Is it the foot?" asked Andy.

"It's not the foot."

"Your head, then."

"It's not the head."

"Then what?"

"It's my sins. I groan for my sins, God forgive me."

"I don't know what you mean."

"Andy, anything that happens from now on will be for your own good. Do you understand what I'm saying?"

"No, I don't understand what you're saying, Vinny. But whatever it is, I don't like the sound of it."

"I only want what's best for you."

Andy waited for him to go on, but he said no more.

"So spit it out, Vinny. What nasty thing is about to happen for my own good?"

"It will be all for the best, remember that."

Andy didn't understand. Vinny was up to something for sure. But what? His head throbbed and his eyes ached and the cockroaches crawled in his belly still. All he knew was that something really bad was about to happen.

When it did happen, it took him completely by surprise.

The light was fading and the rain was coming down heavier than ever and Andy's head was throbbing and his legs felt wobbly, when there came a firm, uncoded knock on the door. The first thing Andy thought of was the police and he wondered if Vinny had managed to get rid of the whiskey, because if he hadn't, then it was more trouble.

"See who it is, Andy."

Andy opened the door.

She was wearing a raincoat, not her long gray coat, but otherwise Aunt Mona looked exactly the same, severe, grim, starchy.

"May I come in?" she said.

"Come in, Mona, come in," Vinny called. He had been stretched out on the sofa, his injured foot resting on the arm, but now he struggled up and slid the whiskey bottle out of sight behind the arm of the sofa.

Aunt Mona stepped inside. "God save all here," she said quietly. She looked at Andy. "Are you ready to go?"

Andy stared at her with burning eyes. He understood. His heart buckled. He turned to Vinny. "You asked her to come and take me," he accused, his voice deadly quiet, head and heart pounding like a pair of drums. "You called her from the hospital!"

Vinny protested, "You don't understand, Andy — "

"You don't want me. That's not hard to understand, Vinny. You're my father, but you don't want me. I hate you!" His father was a traitor. Andy had been betrayed. Stabbed in the back.

"It isn't that I don't want you, Andy, God knows I think the world of you and I'd give anything to keep you, but I can't take care of you here, you know that right well, especially now with these crutches."

"I thought we'd take care of each other," said Andy. "You're my *father*!"

"I am and proud of it. But a boy needs to be looked after properly. And I'm not up to it. It's beyond me. D'you hear what I'm telling you? I'm not the one to bring you up."

"You don't need to bring me up. I can bring myself up."

"You can do no such thing. You're a child. You need a proper home, Andy!"

"I'm your son, Vinny! You're my father! You've *got* to take care of me, not — not *her*! And if you don't think this is a proper home for me, then you've got to find us a proper home, one that *is* good enough!"

Vinny turned to Aunt Mona for help, but she had her back to them, looking out the window. He limped over to Andy and reached out an arm, but Andy backed away.

"Don't touch me! You don't want me!"

"I do want you. When you're gone, it'll be like I've lost an arm and the use of *both* legs. Your aunt is a good woman. She knows what a boy needs. She can take care of you until I'm back on my feet."

"You're full of talk, Vinny. You've got no intention — "

"But I do, Andy! Trust me! I'll not let you down, not this time. Just give me another chance. Leave it to me. But for now, till I find a job and the right place for us, go with your aunt."

"You made promises before."

"I promise on your mother's grave!"

"She's got no — I don't believe you, Vinny. I just don't believe you!"

"Leave everything to me, darlin', I promise."

"You'll get a job?"

"I will."

"And find a proper place?"

"I will."

"You promise?"

"I promise. May God strike me dead if I don't!"

"And you'll send for me right away, as soon as you find it?"

"I will, I swear. God and Mona are my witnesses."

Andy felt a throat swell of despair. He didn't believe Vinny, didn't trust him. He had lied before. Vinny, his father, didn't want him: that was all he could think of. His father didn't want him, and worse still, he'd sent for the one person Andy hated most in all the world: Aunt Mona.

He mumbled to his aunt, "I'll just throw my things in a bag."

They waited for a bus outside the Mayo Rooms. The rain dropped like acid. Andy pulled up the hood of his parka. A nearby garbage can overflowed onto the sidewalk with sodden hamburger cartons, paper cups, cigarette packages, bus tickets, chewing gum wrappers. Someone had thrown up in the gutter. Aunt Mona held an umbrella over them both. They said nothing to each other. Andy stared down the empty gray road. It was too early for the streetlights to come on, but the gray gloom and drizzling rain made it difficult to see far. His head throbbed; he started to shiver. His new parka was warm enough, but this was a chill that began on the inside, in the marrow of his bones, and spread outward to muscle and tissue.

A sudden frightening gust of wind howled at them from nowhere. It blew Mona's umbrella inside out and blew the garbage can over. The filth from the can flew up into the air and landed in a heap about Aunt Mona's feet.

"Well, I never!" she gasped, backing away and hanging on to her broken umbrella.

The air seemed charged with electrical energy. The garbage can rolled about noisily on the sidewalk. Then the wind disappeared as suddenly as it had come and the garbage can was still.

Aunt Mona said quickly, "We'll walk. It's not far." They started walking. Aunt Mona raised the damaged umbrella above their heads. She said, "Are you all right?"

Andy didn't answer her.

"This is all for the best, you'll see," said Aunt Mona. They walked together in silence, Andy trembling in a fever of despair, walking like a robot for what seemed like ten miles under the umbrella through the rain along one poor street and down another to a narrow street of dismal houses. There was a number on Aunt Mona's front door, but to Andy everything was a blur. Aunt Mona opened the door with a key and they went inside.

the aunt

16

HE SLEPT WARMLY through the last few days of November and the first light snow of the year. The room smelled faintly of roses and he was reminded of his mother. Shadowy figures shuffled in and out, bringing water he couldn't swallow without it spilling and pills that stuck in his throat. He was in the hospital again, with nurses coming and going and Father Coughlan murmuring at him about being strong and keeping his faith, but after a while he realized there were only two people, a man and a woman, whispering in drowsy murmurs over him in the language of bees.

He woke in the night and the voices were not there. The room was dark. He tried getting out of the bed, but was too weak, and his head fell back on the pillow. He lay awake, eyes open in the dark. Again, he tried to sit up and swing his legs out from under the covers, but fell back into sleep instead and dreamed about his mother.

Another day. He half woke in the warm room, voices whispering.

He dreamed he was in Tir Na n'Og under a cloudless blue sky in a blue and yellow field — bluebells and buttercups. White horses grazed nearby. His mother was calling him from their tree house, telling him something he couldn't quite hear. Vinny came out of the house, looking like Tarzan. He stood behind Judith, she now in her Jane outfit. Andy started running toward them, but Tarzan lifted Jane with one arm and leaped up to a thick hanging vine, and the two figures swung away into the jungle without him.

He woke and stared at the cracks in the ceiling. The room was dim and quiet. He was alone.

His mother was gone.

And his father didn't want him.

He closed his eyes and sank again into darkness.

Someone sitting near the bed, head bent: a man writing in a newspaper, working on a crossword puzzle. Andy closed his eyes and listened to the man quietly whispering words to his pencil. Then he slept again.

He tried to sit up to take some soup from one of the whisperers, who turned out to be Aunt Mona. When he saw who it was, he said, "I don't want any," and pushed the spoon away.

"Eat. It's good for you."

"I don't care."

129

The second whisperer was the crossword puzzle man. He tiptoed into the room one daylight time and said something Andy did not understand. Andy stared at him, and soon he went away, closing the door quietly behind him.

Another time. Aunt Mona brought food on a tray and sat on the edge of the bed urging him to eat, but he turned his head away and closed his eyes until he heard her leave the room, and then he saw the food left on the tray and ate a little of it, not noticing what it was he was eating. Then he slept again.

The man came in and stood beside the bed.

Andy didn't look at him.

"Hello, Andy. I'm Hugh Hogan."

Andy looked at him. The crossword puzzle man. He was short and barrel-chested, with a shy smile and bristly gray hair like a brush.

"How're you feeling?"

"What's the matter with me?"

"You had the fever."

The fever. He felt empty.

"Mona asked me to look in on you. Are you warm enough?"

He sank back on heaped pillows, closing his eyes. The man left, shutting the door noiselessly behind him. The bed was warm and soft. He slept again.

He woke when Aunt Mona came in with a pink hot-water bottle and tray of food. She put the tray down on the floor and reached under the bedcovers and pulled out another hot-water bottle, this one blue, and held up the pink one for Andy to see. "Do you need another?"

He had never used a hot-water bottle before. "No."

Aunt Mona left it aside and picked up the tray. There was a boiled egg with buttered toast. She placed the tray in front of Andy and perched on the edge of the bed like a bird to watch him eat. He was hungry. He ate.

"That's the first bit of solid food you've got down you in four days," said Aunt Mona. "You're thin as a twig." She saw him glancing around the room. "This is your room now. Your things are in the wardrobe. And extra blankets if you need them. Don't get up until you're ready. You've all the time in the world." She took the tray when Andy was finished, and stood. "I'll bring you up some milk."

When his aunt had gone back downstairs with the tray and the blue hot-water bottle, he slipped out of bed on wobbly legs, grabbed the pink hot-water bottle, and took it into bed with him and slipped it under his thighs. It was too hot, so he slid it down toward the bottom of the bed near his feet. After a while he got up again and walked shakily to the window and looked out. Snow, everything covered thinly in snow. It was early morning, he could tell by the hazy brightness of the sky over the roofs of the houses. He was looking down on a small backyard. The neighbors on either side had identical yards, separated by snow-topped fences, and across the cobbled alleyway were duplicate yards repeated monotonously along the row of houses. Most, including Aunt Mona's, had lines hung with washing that fluttered fitfully in the wind. There was a cold draft. He looked up; the top part of the window was open. He reached up and pushed it closed.

He turned and looked about him. He had the small room to himself, upstairs at the back of the house. The room was warm, but he shivered and wrapped his arms about himself. The floor was wood and the wallpaper was an ugly lemon color with a sucky white butterflies-and-daisies design. The bed had a thick mattress, white sheets, creamy blankets, an old faded lemon candlewick bed-spread, and several heavy, plump pillows in white cotton pillowcases. The room's furniture included a plain var-nished chair; a small, ugly chest of drawers, varnished, with a fussy white lace runner, an old-fashioned alarm clock, and a calendar on it; a tall and ugly wooden closet — what his aunt had called the wardrobe — with an oval mirror on its door set in a wood frame; a framed picture hanging on the wall near the door of Jesus pointing to His bleeding heart; and a red throw rug on the wood floor between the bed and the chest. The time on the alarm clock was twenty after six. Beside the bed was a small table. There were no bookshelves in the room, no radio. Everything was clean, polished. A light with a frosted glass shade on it dangled from the ceiling center. It was the only light in the room. The switch was next to the bleeding-heart picture. He hated the bleeding-heart picture and hated the room.

He remembered Vinny's words: "I'll find the right place for us. Leave it to me."

His father wanted him. Of course his father wanted him. He had promised to find a place for them both. He had promised to send for him.

Vinny *did* want him; he had to believe that.

He looked around the room; it would do as a temporary solution, until his father sent for him. Or until his mother came for him.

He discovered himself in the mirror. Pale puffy face. Eyes black like … raisins. He was wearing cotton pajamas, obviously new; he couldn't remember putting them on. He opened the closet doors and saw his parka on a hanger, and his jeans. There were drawers in the lower part of the closet, all empty. The top of the drawers formed a shelf, upon which were two folded blankets. He found his shirts, pants, socks, a second pair of pajamas in the chest of drawers, everything clean and folded. The floor was cold on his bare feet, so he rolled back into the warm bed and sat with his feet on the hot-water bottle and the covers pulled up to his chin. He studied the cracks on the ceiling. Could his mother see him now?

He remembered leaving the Mayo Rooms with Aunt Mona, remembered Vinny's face, like the face of the suffering Jesus over on the wall. Andy slid out of bed quickly, lifted the bleeding-heart picture down off the wall, and laid it facedown in the bottom drawer of the chest. Then he got back into bed again, closed his eyes, and slept.

When he woke, the room was dark except for silver moonbeams angling through the window. He saw the Sheehogue sitting on the windowsill in the bright moonlight, four of them, kicking their legs up in the air and laughing and arguing in Little People language. They wore tiny Moosehead hockey shirts, and their hair grew straight on their tiny heads like unmown grass.

One of them noticed him watching and waved. "Hello, Andy."

"Hello, Andy!" they all called to him.

He tried to wave back but couldn't lift his arm. Then he saw a fifth, an old white-bearded one in a plain green collarless shirt, lying at the foot of his bed, bathed in moonlight, sleeping with his mouth wide open, cuddled up against the pink hot-water bottle. Andy tried to keep his eyes open so he could continue to watch them, but he fell asleep.

When next he woke, it was still dark outside but the room light was on. The windowsill and bed were empty of Little People. Like Tarzan and Jane, it had been just another dream.

Aunt Mona came in, after knocking, with food on a tray. She set the tray on the side table. "I've brought you some soup."

"I don't like soup."

"Good food means good health. You must eat to keep up your strength." She moved the chair closer to the bed and sat facing Andy, waiting for him to help himself to the food, but he ignored the tray, glaring at her. The thing he always noticed first about his aunt was her eyes, bright, dark, penetrating, as if she could see into him and read his thoughts. She wore a long blue skirt, cream blouse, and dark blue cardigan. She smelled of rose water. She looked and smelled different without the mothballed gray armor of her coat, serious and stern as usual, but softer somehow, more natural and relaxed, shoulders and neck not so stiff, younger perhaps, for though cut severely, her thick black hair showed only a few strands of gray, and the pinched gray face that Andy remembered from the taxi as they rode to the airport now appeared pinkly normal, so that she didn't seem any older than his mother.

Aunt Mona said, "It's stuffy in here." She noticed the closed window. "Fresh air is food for the lungs." She got up, opened the window, and then sat again. "Would you like another hot-water — "

"I don't want to stay here. My father will take care of me as soon as he's better."

"Your father! Hmmph! That man can't even take care of himself. You'll be looked after properly here, I promise you. Good plain food, and a bath every day whether you think you need it or not. Merciful heaven! I thought it was a chimney sweep I was looking at when I came for you on Friday. Your hair was black with filth and you smelled so bad it made my eyes smart. There's no excuse for dirt. You couldn't have been dirtier if you'd come straight from a factory chimney. And thin? Like a darning needle! You must have eaten nothing all the time you were there. It's no wonder you were sick."

Andy glared at her.

"Your father hasn't the faintest idea of how to bring up a child. And even if he did, he wouldn't have the time;

he's too fond of his friends and his gambling and his drink."

"You're always saying horrible lies about my father! He's a good man and he wants me! And I don't need anyone to bring me up; I'm eleven and I can bring myself up." Andy glared defiantly at his aunt.

"I've no wish to fight with you, boy, but I'm a plainspoken woman, inclined to be abrupt — some might say blunt. Eat the soup I brought you. You need building up." She stood and took a blanket from the closet. "The heat doesn't seem to get up to this room much. I'll throw an extra blanket over the bed."

"I don't need it. And I don't need your soup."

She dropped the blanket onto the chair. "It'll be there should you want it." She marched to the door. "And you might change your mind about the soup. By the way, your Aunt Jill and Uncle Joe are coming to dinner on Sunday. Jill is Hugh's sister, so she isn't really your aunt, not a blood relative, I mean. Nor is Joe really your uncle. But you're family; they think of you as a nephew: they're looking forward to meeting Judith's boy."

"Did my father phone to see how ..."

She hesitated. Then, "No."

"Are you sure?"

Aunt Mona's voice softened. "Yes, I'm sure." She thought for a second. "Probably can't get to a phone because of his crutches."

As soon as his aunt had left, Andy spread the blanket on the bed and tried the soup. It seemed okay; he was hungry, so finished it off, then stared at the empty bowl. His mother was gone. I'm Vinny's boy now, not Judith's, Vinny's. Poor old Vinny, limping along on crutches. He would go see how his father was, as soon as he felt okay again. If his aunt tried to stop him, he'd go anyway.

"The home is warm and comfortable," observed a Young One.

"With excellent care," admitted another.

"And good food."

"Then there is definitely no need for us to stay any longer."

"Not another day."

"Not yet," said the Old One.

"But in the name of Cuchulainn, why not?"

"Wait and see."

17

DAYLIGHT. Uncle Hugh knocked on the door, bringing him an orange. "Your vitamin C," he said with a shy smile. "Mona asked me to bring it up."

Andy pulled himself up to a sitting position.

"Will I peel it for you?" He sat on the chair with its back against the wall, and started peeling the orange with a penknife.

Andy watched his uncle's big hands. "Whose room was this before I came?"

His uncle's bristly gray eyebrows knotted together. "It was Mother Costello's, before she got too old to climb the stairs. It hasn't been used in years." His voice was soft and slow, with a whispery Irish burr to it.

"Is Mother Costello my grandmother?"

"She is."

"Is she in an old folks' home?"

He smiled. "You'd never get that one in a home. No, she has the front room. You'll meet her when you're able to come down."

Andy looked around. "Did you paint this room?"

"I did."

"And wallpapered it?"

He nodded. " 'A boy cares how his room is,' Mona said. Everything had to be right. But it was herself who picked out the paint color and the paper pattern." He chuckled. "'I wouldn't trust a Galway man to pick the paper for a pigsty,' she said. D'you like it, then?"

He didn't answer. Chosen by his aunt. Stupid butterflies. He might have known.

"She had the room done special for you coming."

"I'm only here on a temporary basis, until my father comes for me; I hope you realize that."

His face fell. "Temporary basis is it? Well ..." He stretched across the empty space and handed Andy the peeled orange in a paper towel. Then he wiped the blade of the penknife with a second paper towel, folded the blade, and pushed it into the pocket of his corduroy trousers. He had short, thick fingers. "Well," he said again and slapped his knees with the palms of his hands, preparing to stand and go.

"Thanks."

His uncle was still sitting. He was trying to say something. His blue eyes widened with the effort. "Andy, I just want you to know ... you're very welcome here." He paused awkwardly. "More than welcome."

Andy said nothing.

"We never had children, y'see," he continued quietly. "Mona made novenas galore and Stations of the Cross and

prayed to St. Theresa and St. Jude and had a dozen mass-
es said for our private intention, but" — he shook his head
— "it wasn't meant to be. When your mother ... when she
... when you were alone in Vancouver, in the hospital,
Mona lit a candle every morning to the Blessed Virgin
Mary, above at the church, that you'd be happy here."

As if realizing he'd talked too much, the shyness came
over him again and he slapped and dusted his corduroy
knees that didn't need dusting and stood and went to the
door. He looked back at Andy with a smile, then closed the
door behind him.

Granny Costello was very old.

Andy studied her. This was his mother's mother. And
Aunt Mona's mother. She had skin the yellow color of a
Spanish onion, and she sat in a special electric lounger
with a rug over her in front of the TV in the living room.
The chair had a button on the arm, and when Granny
touched it the seat tilted backward or forward electrically
and slowly, so that if she needed to sleep she kept her
thumb on the button until it settled back as far as she
wanted, and if she needed to get up for anything the chair
ejected her gently forward onto her feet. She didn't walk
unless she had to. When she needed to get up, she hobbled
and had to be taken by the arm and helped. She ate very
tiny meals in her chair from a special tray and watched TV
or dozed all day.

When Aunt Mona tried to introduce Andy to her,
Granny was absorbed in a soap opera. Her bright black

lizard eyes gleamed. She pointed to the TV. "*Coronation Street,*" she snapped at Mona.

"Yes, Mother," Mona snapped back. "But this is Andy."

Andy could see who his aunt took after.

"Andy?" Granny Costello said slowly, frowning, trying to remember.

"Andy Flynn," said Aunt Mona in a louder voice. She picked up the remote and switched off the sound. "Judith's boy."

Granny fiddled with the volume control of her hearing aid. "Did you say Judith?" Her face lit up and she smiled a beautiful smile at Andy. "Judith?" She sounded even more Irish than Aunt Mona.

Aunt Mona leaned over her mother. "It's Judith's boy; it's Andy," she said patiently. "He's come to live with us, remember I told you?"

"Live with us?" Granny Costello looked pleased. "That's very nice indeed. Judith's boy." She thought for a few seconds and then said, "Judith went away to ... Where did she go, Mona?"

"Vancouver," said Aunt Mona.

"Where?"

"British Columbia. The West Coast."

"That's it. She left. We told her not to go. It's a big mistake, leaving the ones who love you most." She frowned and shook her head. "We asked her not to go," she said to Andy. "And if the truth be known, I don't think her heart was really in it. But she did love that husband of hers, that nice young whatsisname. I'd follow him to the ends of the earth, she said. Seems to me I remember I had a soft spot for whatsisname myself. I told him, I told whatsisname, if I was forty years younger, I told him, I'd — " She broke off, then brightly, to Andy, "Do you own a motorcycle?"

Andy said, "No."

"What a pity. Perhaps one day you will own one and we can go for a ride." She craned her skinny neck and offered her withered cheek. Andy, still a bit wobbly in the legs, leaned down carefully and brushed her cheek with his lips. She smelled like mushrooms.

The house was small, with boxy rooms. The living room was so cluttered with dark polished bits and pieces of furniture that it was difficult to walk about. There was a fireplace with logs stacked. Granny's TV, a black monster, seemed to take up most of the space. The telephone was in the hallway near the front door. In the kitchen there was a small fridge and a gas stove and a pair of small apartment-size laundry machines, but no dishwasher or microwave. Aunt Mona and Uncle Hugh shared the only other bedroom, upstairs next to Andy's. The bathroom had an old iron tub with claw feet and no shower and was on the upstairs landing, three steps down from the bedrooms. When Andy needed a bath, he switched on the heater and waited a few minutes until the water was hot. But the bathroom was clean; unlike the Mayo's, it gleamed and had plenty of soap and toilet paper and bright fluffy towels. Granny slept downstairs in the front room, which Aunt Mona called the parlor, next to the living room. Andy wondered how the old lady managed if she needed to go to the bathroom during the night. He soon found out one afternoon when Granny, watching the TV in the living room as usual, called out in a high, fluting voice, "Toilet, Mona!" and Aunt Mona helped her hobble to a downstairs toilet, a tiny room near the stairs, that Andy hadn't noticed.

Though Uncle Hugh was not a tall man, he was wide across the chest and shoulders and his neck was thick with muscle. He worked for the brewery, in the loading bay, he told Andy, and smelled of hops and barley. Andy liked Uncle Hugh and his malty smell. His quiet, welcoming acceptance of Andy calmed him, helped him feel more comfortable in the old house with his starchy aunt and dotty old granny.

He missed Vinny.

Aunt Mona told him he would have to make his own bed and keep his room clean, and when he was feeling stronger there would be household jobs for him to do.

"Do you mean chores?" asked Andy.

"Jobs," said Mona.

"Like what?"

"Don't worry," said Aunt Mona. "There's always plenty to do. I'll show you how to hang the wash out on the line and bring it in when it's dry. That's one little job. There'll be others, too, like clearing snow. But only when you're strong enough. No hurry. There's all the time in the world for you to build up your strength."

"Jobs!" Andy muttered to himself.

Old cow.

Aunt Mona reminded him that Hugh's sister and her husband were coming on Sunday. "The girl will be coming, too," she said, "their daughter, Una."

"Is she my cousin?"

"Not really. An almost cousin. Una, is eleven, same as yourself."

Andy liked the idea of having an almost cousin, especially one his own age. But he was apprehensive. The thought of these strangers coming just to meet him was unsettling. He imagined them studying him closely, searching for indications of who-knew-what deficiency or family weakness. How much did they know about Vinny? he wondered.

Or would they feel sorry for him? He imagined them saying to one another, "Poor thing." And, "What a desperate shame."

If Vinny didn't keep his promise and fix things so he could get away from Aunt Mona, he would hate him forever and ever and ever.

18

"DID YOU SAY YOUR PRAYERS?" Aunt Mona asked briskly, sweeping into the room after a rapid knock, carrying a hot-water bottle and bringing with her the faintest scent of roses. It was the smell he remembered from his fever, and from his mother.

"Yeah," he lied. He was reading *Watership Down* in bed, a pretty good story about a bunch of rabbits; he'd found it on the shelves in the hallway. Aunt Mona said it belonged to Una.

"D'you want the hot-water bottle?"

"No."

"I'll leave it at the foot of the bed so." Aunt Mona fussed with the quilt. "Did you say a prayer for your granny and Uncle Hugh?"

"Mmnn."

"And your mother?"

"Mmnn."

"And your poor unfortunate father?"

"My father's not unfortunate."

"Good night, then. God bless."

When his aunt had gone he pulled the hot-water bottle into the bed.

Aunt Mona explained how to get there. "Ten minutes if you walk quickly. The rain has melted most of the snow, but I'll give you the bus fare in case you need it. The bus takes only a few minutes."

It was Saturday morning. Andy took the money but walked through cold streets. By the time he got to the Mayo Rooms, his legs were tired and his feet hurt. Sickness and lack of exercise had made him weak. He would have to toughen up for soccer; there was no way he could sprint down the left wing with the ball glued to his foot in his present condition.

He stood outside the Mayo and looked up. The familiar spectacles stared back at him as if to say, "What? You again? We thought we'd got rid of you." He went in and climbed the stairs and tried Vinny's door, but it was locked. He knocked. Silence. Vinny had gone out early. Or hadn't come home, more like.

He hadn't brought his key, so sat on the stairs and waited for about an hour. No Vinny. Outside, the rain was starting. He zipped up his parka and took the bus back to Aunt Mona's.

Andy went to mass at St. Gregory's with his uncle and aunt on Sunday morning, his aunt sternly armored in her long gray coat. She walked briskly with her head high, looking neither left nor right, dark eyes haughty and composed. Uncle Hugh's muscular neck looked uncomfortable in a shirt and tie. He gave Andy his missal. "It's yours if you'd like to keep it," he said. "The print is too small for me to read even if I wanted to."

The mass droned on; Andy listened to very little of the sermon. But he liked the color pictures in the missal his uncle had given him, and he liked its weight. And he liked the crowd of people, their murmured responses, and the chance to stretch in the standings and kneelings, and the hymns, and the smell of the incense, and the high stained-glass windows with the red, blue, green light pouring through the images of the saints. The smiling Jesus carrying a white lamb in His arms reminded Andy of how much he had always longed for a dog. If Aunt Mona would let him have a dog, then he could take it with him when he moved back with his father. He leaned sideways and whispered urgently, "Uncle Hugh?"

His uncle bent his head.

"Do you think I could have a pup?"

Uncle Hugh frowned. "Huh?"

"A dog?"

"I could ask Mona," he whispered.

"Would you? Please?"

"Shush!" said Aunt Mona.

The guests arrived before noon. Dinner was at one. Uncle Hugh's sister, Jill, had Andy in a bear hug before she'd taken off her coat. For a small woman, she had a strong hugging apparatus. She had lively gray eyes and curly hair held up with combs. "Call me Jill," she told him. Aunt Mona and Uncle Hugh stood back quietly, Aunt Mona stern and haughty as usual, Uncle Hugh with his shy smile.

"And this is Joe," Jill said, introducing her husband.

"Hello, Andy," said Joe, shaking his hand, smiling. "Welcome to Halifax." Joe, short and slim, had thinning brown hair and brown eyes, and a gap between his two top teeth.

"And this is Una," said Jill.

Una was pretty, with her mother's gray eyes, and brown hair chopped cleanly at the jawline. She just waved a hand. "Hi," she said casually.

"Why don't you take Una over to the playground," Aunt Mona suggested to Andy. "Dinner won't be for an hour yet."

They strolled over to the playground, acting cool, saying very little, and sat on a pair of swings, dangling together, burying the toes of their shoes in the wet sand, still saying very little. The girls Andy had known in Vancouver giggled a lot and chattered together like birds in a tree. Una seemed quiet and sensible.

"I'm reading your book," Andy said, just to get things started. "It's pretty good."

"Which one's that?"

"*Watership Down.*"

"Isn't it great? I love animal stories. I'm reading a new book called *White as the Waves*, all about whales. One of them is Moby Dick; he's the one who's white. It is so great. I'll let you have it when I'm finished if you like."

"Thanks."

Una wanted to know if there were grizzly bears in British Columbia. And what about cougars? "I plan to be a veterinarian," she confided. "What are you going to be?"

"Famous soccer player," Andy said. "And if I can't be that, then I want to work in the circus or the movies as an animal trainer. Animal trainers are well paid, and, of course, you get to work with all kinds of animals. But that's only if I don't play pro soccer."

"Fate," said Una. "I knew we'd have lots in common. But wouldn't it be awfully dangerous training circus animals, like lions and tigers?"

Andy shrugged. "Looking them in the eye is really important, and letting them see who's boss."

Una said, "Lions are interesting. Did you know that the life span of a lion in the wild is only about twelve years, but a lion in captivity lives to be thirty?"

"I didn't know that."

"I read it in my lion book." She stopped swinging and looked into Andy's eyes. "If you were a lion and had a choice of living in the wild for twelve years or living in captivity for thirty, which do you think you'd choose?"

Andy thought for a second. "I'd choose the wild."

"So would I," said Una, her serious face easing into a luminous smile.

They hooked elbows around the cold chains and swung together in contented silence for a while.

"What's your school like?" Andy asked.

"St. Gregory's? It's okay." Una pulled a face. "If you can stand the boredom. Being in school is a bit like being a lion in captivity, don't you think? If it were not for my friends I'd probably go barking mad. Will you be starting tomorrow?"

"Aunt Mona hasn't said anything, but I'd like to go. It'll only be temporary, of course, till my father finds a new place and comes for me, and then I'll probably go someplace else, to St. Dominic's maybe, and get a place on the soccer team."

"Oh." Una looked disappointed. "I was hoping we might be friends. Why aren't you living with your father?"

"You don't know?"

Una shook her head. She didn't look to Andy like the kind of girl who told lies. She was easy to talk to. He liked her.

A breeze sprang up and the third swing, empty beside them, began swinging. Soon it was spinning and bouncing, its chains clinking and rattling. Andy and Una watched in surprise.

"Halifax winds are sure crazy," said Andy.

They watched until the swing stopped its twisted leaping and became still.

"I thought I heard wind chimes," said Una.

Andy grinned. "It's probably the Little People." He told her about Vinny and his stories. "In Ireland they're called the Sheehogue. Vinny used to tell me stories about them when I was little. The Little People interfere in people's lives sometimes, making mischief mostly. Vinny says they do good to the good and evil to the evil."

"Tell me a Little People story."

So he did. He told her first of all about Tir Na n'Og, the place of eternal youth, and then he told how Lord Fitzgerald fell in love with an orphan girl. When he was finished, Una sighed. "Do you believe people can love one another forever and beyond, Andy?"

Andy had to admit he didn't really know.

"I don't see why not," said Una. "It's terribly romantic!" Her brow wrinkled in thought. "Eternal love is lovely. And Tir Na n'Og sounds like a beautiful place." She thought for a few more seconds. "But I'm not sure if I'd want to live forever and ever, Andy, would you? I'd probably go barking mad."

With seven people in it, the small dining room was crowded.

Confused, and trying to follow the noisy babble, Granny interrupted conversations often to ask, "What was that you said?" or "Could you please speak up a little? I can't hear you." Whenever she did manage to hear something, she exclaimed, "Well, I never!" or "Fancy that!"

Uncle Hugh tapped his glass with a spoon. Everyone was quiet while he said grace. When he was finished, they said "Amen" and reached for their knives and forks, but Uncle Hugh stopped them with "And let us, while we're at it, offer up a prayer for Judith, sorely missed."

"May she rest in peace," came the response.

"And Andy's stepfather," Mona reminded Hugh, "even though we didn't know the poor man."

"Rest in peace."

"And finally," said Uncle Hugh, smiling shyly over at Andy, "let us say a prayer of thanks for bringing us Andy."

"Welcome," and "Thanks be to God," they murmured as they crossed themselves, and looked at Andy, and smiled.

The noisy babble started up again. Andy tried to follow what people were saying. The guests were interested in him, Jill overwhelming him with questions about school in Vancouver, his stay in the hospital, his hobbies, what he thought about his courageous Aunt Mona flying all that way over the country, east to west and back again, five miles up in the sky, she who had never set foot in an airplane in her whole life, who had a mortal dread of heights, who had trembled with fear through every minute of the flight, the poor, brave woman.

Just as Andy was digesting this last piece of information, Joe asked him from across the table, "How do you like living in Halifax, Andy?"

"Fine," Andy answered, though he was still thinking about Aunt Mona.

Trembled? Fear? Aunt Mona trembling with fear?

Nobody mentioned Vinny.

"I haven't got my glasses," Granny said to Joe beside her. "What's this on my plate?"

Joe took her hand and guided her fork on a tour around the plate. "This is a roast potato," he explained patiently, "chopped into pieces. This is roast lamb, cut up. Here on the side is some mashed turnip and parsnip, and this is broccoli, just a bit. You have no mint sauce; shall I pour some on your lamb?"

"Thank you, Joseph."

Andy sat opposite Una, who glanced at him frequently and smiled, as though they shared an important secret.

19

"YOU'RE WELL ENOUGH to start school tomorrow," said Aunt Mona later that evening, after the guests had gone.

"I don't want to go to school here. I'll wait till Vin — till I'm with my father."

"St. Gregory's is strict, mind, but a bit of discipline never harmed anyone, in my view."

"I don't want to go to St. Gregory's." He knew he was being contrary. He didn't mention that, starved of friendship, he was looking forward to seeing Una again.

"You will go to school and that's the end of it," said Aunt Mona in her no-nonsense voice. "There will be no argument. If you like, I will come with you on your first day."

"I can go on my own."

"As you wish."

When he got home from school after his first day, Aunt Mona asked, "Well? How did you like it?"

Andy shrugged. "It was okay." He didn't tell her it was

actually pretty good; it was great to be with kids his own age again instead of walking idly around the downtown, bored out of his mind. And there had been talk of a soccer team.

"I left a bit of pocket money on your dresser."

"Thanks, but I won't need it. My father will be taking care of things like that."

"Your father!" Aunt Mona's dark eyes flashed.

"Yes, my father. You don't need to say it so nasty."

"I wasn't being nasty. But if you're waiting for your father to come for you, then you might be waiting till the snakes return to Ireland."

"He said he'd find us a place and he will. I trust him even if you don't!"

"No, Andy, I don't trust him. He's a storyteller and a liar. He'd break your heart, that man. I don't like to see you pinning your hopes on him. He'll only hurt you, child."

"I won't listen to you! You've always hated him."

"I hate no man."

Andy flung himself away from her.

Old cow.

"Before you start any homework," she called after him, "I would like you to fix your room. You left your bed unmade this morning. And there's soiled clothing on the floor. That'll not do. I noticed, too, that the sheets need washing. Please put them in the laundry basket on the landing and take a clean set from the airing cupboard. Cleanliness is next to godliness."

Old witch! Andy thought to himself as he started up the stairs.

"Andy!" Aunt Mona calling him back.

She could read his mind; how could he have forgotten?

"Andy, sit down for a minute." She pulled a chair out from the kitchen table for him to sit. "I want to tell you something about your father."

"I don't believe anything you say!"

"Listen to me for just a minute."

He perched himself on the edge of the chair, ready to get up and run if she said one mean thing.

"I do *not* hate your father." She pierced him with her black eyes. "You've got to know that. I've called him some terrible things, like a thief and liar, but he wasn't always like that. When your father was a young man, when he was courting your mother, we all loved him. We loved him. And why not? Vincent Flynn was the sweetest young man in all of Halifax, for he never spoke ill of anyone, not even of William Fahey, the monster who lived next door and beat his wife and children when he had the drink in him. Vincent Flynn saw only goodness in the world and he was always cheerful and good-natured, always full of fun, telling the wildest stories, just as he does now, and not a bit of harm in him; he'd give you the last penny in his pocket if you asked for it. Judith loved him. We all did; we thought the world of him, even if he did spend too much time sitting and reading."

Reading? Andy thought to himself. Vinny? The same Vinny who failed kindergarten?

"It was Vincent's only fault. He sat and he sat and he read and he read. He never stopped reading — everything he could lay his hands on, books as thick as his own arm, many of them — when he could've been out sailing with his brother in the fresh air or playing soccer for the brewery team."

"He's got a brother?"

"The pair of them came out from Ireland and got jobs at the brewery. Tim was two years older, a fine boy — they were both fine boys. Tim soon had a wee sailboat — he was mad about sailing. Vincent idolized his brother. Then he met your mother and they couldn't wait to get married. The wedding was in St. Gregory's; the whole neighborhood turned out for it. Tim was the best man. Judith was lovely, the picture of happiness. They hadn't much money, so they drove down the peninsula to Peggy's Cove for their honeymoon. They started their married life in a wee house not far from here, renting and saving so that one day they'd have a house of their own. You were born in that house; I'll show you where it is sometime if you like.

"Tim worked the hoist at the brewery, unloading the trucks that came to the warehouse. He didn't wear his safety belt one day and fell from the sixth-floor loading door to the ground beneath and died in a minute. Vincent was never the same after that; he took to drink and soon lost his job. Then he and Judith went out to Vancouver to try their luck. The rest you know. Your father became his own worst enemy. I'm only telling you this so you'll know how much we loved him, but it was like he, too, died that day when Tim fell and broke his neck. There was no helping your father after that."

Andy started to think over what his aunt had said. But there was too much to grasp.

Aunt Mona cut into his thoughts; she said quietly, "So you see, I do not hate your father. But I lost respect a long time ago for the man he became. Without honor and pride, Vincent Flynn has wasted his life. After Tim died, it was like he gave up on everything. There; that's all I have to say."

Andy wanted to defend his father, but didn't know how. Tears of frustration stung his eyes. He turned his back on his aunt and hurried up the stairs to his room. He needed to be alone; he needed to think.

The next morning, after Aunt Mona had checked Andy's room, she said, "You made a good job of it. I like things nice and clean and tidy." She was making porridge.

"I hate porridge!" he said.

"Then we shall have to get you something else," said Aunt Mona calmly, "something you like, so long as it's not sugar puffs and so long as I approve of it. You can't go to school without a proper breakfast."

"Anything but porridge."

"Leave the porridge aside. I'll do you a brown egg. My neighbor Molly Brannigan has a cousin with a farm and she gets them for me fresh each week."

"I'll be going to Una's on the way home from school."

"Very well, but stay no more than the half hour. Then come home and do your homework; you can always go over again later if there's time, or have her come here."

The rain stopped and the weather got colder. There was frost on Andy's bedroom window. Aunt Mona gave him a hot-water bottle to take up and put in his bed an hour before bedtime every night. He also took down an extra wool blanket off the shelf in the closet and threw it on his bed, a comforting weight.

Uncle Hugh had said nothing about the dog; Andy reckoned he must have forgotten. Or hadn't understood. Or Aunt Mona had said no, more like.

Interfering old busybody.

Old cow.

Another week had gone by without a word from Vinny.

"Are you sure he didn't call?" Andy asked Aunt Mona when he got back one evening after kicking a ball around in the park with a bunch of the kids from school.

"He didn't call."

"Are you sure?"

"Yes, Andy, I'm sure."

"Maybe Uncle Hugh took a message and forgot — "

"Hugh took no message."

Andy went up to his room and lay on the bed in the half darkness, staring up at the cracks in the ceiling.

"I sent word to your father to come for dinner," said Aunt Mona. "Edna Rooney at the Mayo Rooms passed on my message."

Andy said nothing. He hadn't heard from Vinny in three weeks. They were sitting in the living room, talking about Christmas. It was getting late, and Andy's eyes felt heavy; he had already put the hot-water bottle in his bed and he would soon have to climb the stairs. Uncle Hugh was doing the daily crossword, reading glasses perched on the end of his nose; Aunt Mona was darning Uncle Hugh's socks; Granny had fallen asleep watching the news.

"That'll be lovely," said Uncle Hugh. He looked up and smiled at Andy.

"Off to bed with you, then," Aunt Mona said to Andy. "I'll come up in a few minutes to say good night."

20

AUNT MONA HELD CHRISTMAS DINNER BACK for over an hour, waiting for him to come, but when he hadn't shown by two o'clock, they went ahead without him. Aunt Mona shrugged her shoulders. "If I didn't know him as well as I do, I'd be as mad as a bag of cats," was all she said.

The table was set for five, the empty place like a gap in a hedge.

"We'll save him a plate in the oven," said Uncle Hugh. "He might come yet."

He wouldn't come; Andy knew Vinny wouldn't come; he'd be too busy, or he'd forget, or he'd be unconscious in bed from a long night out with his friends. He sneaked a glance at his new digital watch, from Mona and Hugh.

"Who is coming?" Gran wanted to know for the second time in ten minutes.

"Andy's father," said Uncle Hugh.

"Do I know him?" asked Granny.

"He and Judith went away to the west," answered Aunt Mona.

"Who?"

"Vincent," said Aunt Mona patiently. "Vincent Flynn."

"Of course I remember him," said Granny. "Whatsisname. Vincent. He was Judith's young man; he made me laugh, and had the loveliest tenor voice — sang 'Kathleen, Mavourneen' like an angel — and brought me flowers on my birthday." She turned to Andy, smiling fondly. "I've always had a soft spot for Vincent."

They started on their turkey dinner, Andy helping Gran chop her meat and potatoes into bite-sized pieces, trying not to let his disappointment show. He only toyed with his own food. Aunt Mona and Uncle Hugh were almost finished when a knock came on the door.

Vinny!

They went to the door to let him in. Andy's heart leaped up at the sight of his father's smiling face.

"Merry Christmas," he said to Andy, kissing his cheek and giving his shoulder a squeeze. "God save all here," he said to Aunt Mona and Uncle Hugh. "And a Merry Christmas."

No crutches. Though he'd shaved and had brushed his hair, he still looked the same: old raincoat, stained sweater, old frayed cords, battered shoes silvered from age, rain, snow, and neglect. A small new scar decorated his temple.

"Merry Christmas," they answered, greeting Vinny in their own ways: Uncle Hugh with a handshake and a quiet smile; Aunt Mona, with a starchy look of truce to make it plain that just because it was Christmas didn't mean she was about to change her opinion of him, but following it up with a friendly enough greeting.

They moved into the house, Uncle Hugh with his arm around Vinny's thin shoulders. Vinny laughed. "Sorry if I'm a bit late. You'd never believe the troubles I had getting here. There was the terrible accident with the bus running over a rabbit — "

"There are no rabbits on the streets of Halifax," Aunt Mona snapped.

Vinny hung his coat in the hall. "Merry Christmas, Ma," he shouted in at Granny when he saw her seated at the table.

"Who are you?" asked Granny.

"Vincent Flynn, Ma; you remember your favorite son-in-law surely?"

"Vincent? Is it you?" Granny tried to get up out of her chair but was so excited she forgot to press her ejection button and floundered helplessly instead. "What a lovely surprise!" she said. "Where have you been? Come and give an old lady a kiss, you bad boy." She held out her arms and Vincent kissed her enthusiastically and noisily on both cheeks.

"My, this *is* nice." Granny beamed happily at everyone.

"Was it killed?" asked Andy anxiously. "The rabbit?"

"Ah! It was. There was nothing anyone could do to save the poor creature. It hopped out from the pet shop and under the wheels of the bus. Wasn't it as flat as a pancake there in the middle of the road? With its homogoblin splattered all over the wheel of the bus? There was an old

163

woman sitting in the front seat who saw the whole thing, and she was screaming and yelling for an ambylance when any eejit could see you'd need a spatula to pick the unfortunate beast up off the road. 'Its vital life signs are terrible low,' I tells her — trying to calm her down, you understand? And then we're no sooner back on the bus than the same old woman who'd been yelling for an ambylance, and who hauls herself gasping to the back of the bus so she won't be asked to bear witness to the violent death of a fellow mammal, ups and collapses into the aisle of the bus with a heart attack. It was a great commotion, so it was, with the driver running about like an American basketball star, and the passengers shouting and screaming for someone to phone for the doctor and the ambylance. 'The rabbit was a sign!' a little man in front of me yells. 'Be quiet, you!' I tell him, and I kneel down in the aisle beside the poor dying woman, and I give her mouth-to-mouth recitation until the ambylance comes. They lift her up onto the stretcher and she gives a sigh and starts breathing again. 'You saved her life!' says the little man. The bus driver shakes me by the hand and has them all singing 'For he's a jolly good feller' as we take off once again, and they kept up the singing all the way down to the end of the road where I got off; can you believe such a mad journey as I've had this day?"

"No," said Aunt Mona, her patience almost exhausted with having to listen to such a long rigmarole. "I don't believe a word of your country bumpkin story. You were drinking in Noonan's and you forgot the time."

Uncle Hugh laughed. "It's hard to believe, right enough, but sit down and I'll pour you a drink."

"It's lovely to see you, Andy!" Vinny hugged him and kissed him again. "Lookit! The red cheeks on him and the eyes sparkling with health!" He laughed. "Is it in Tir Na n'Og you are, Andy? Did the Faeries steal you away from me altogether?"

He had brought nothing with him. Andy didn't care; his father was here, that was all that mattered.

"Here, Dad, I got you these." He handed him a big bag of raisins. Dad; he was finished calling him Vinny. It would always be Dad from now on.

He was delighted. "That's grand, Andy," he said. "There's enough here to keep me out of harm's way for a whole year."

His dad enjoyed the roast turkey. There were roast potatoes, too, and stuffing and green peas and brussels sprouts. Hugh slipped Andy a half glass of wine when Mona wasn't looking. Andy had never had wine before; it made him feel dizzy; he liked it. Uncle Hugh said a drink once a year would do no harm. Vincent Flynn made a toast to everyone's health.

"Good health," Granny repeated.

"We'll all drink to that," said Uncle Hugh, touching his glass to Granny's and Aunt Mona's, then Andy's and his father's.

When dinner was over, Aunt Mona and Uncle Hugh started cleaning up in the kitchen.

"I'll help," Andy offered.

"No, Andy," said Aunt Mona. "You go in and talk to your father. It's a while since you saw him. There must be lots for you to talk about."

His father had helped himself to the wine and was sitting back comfortably near the fire, smoking a cigarette.

"How much longer do I have to stay here, Dad? Did you get a job yet?"

"I saw a man in maintenance at the Metro Centre; he thinks he can get me in. So keep your fingers crossed. You'll not be here long, Andy, you'll see." He smiled his tilted smile, his eyes dancing with good humor. "We'll soon be together again. Leave it to me."

"Dad? Could you call me? I know you don't have a phone, but there's one in the manager's office you could use. Just so I know you're all right."

"Of course I will, Andy. I don't know why I didn't think of it. I'm not much of a one for telephones, as you know, but I'll call you for sure."

"Sundays maybe, in the evening. Could you do that?"

"Leave it to me."

Much later, after Vincent Flynn had said his goodbyes to Hugh and Mona, Andy stood with him outside on the street. He gripped Andy's shoulders and gave them a squeeze, struggling to say something, but then he squeezed his shoulders one last time and turned quickly away. Andy watched him hurry up the street, tilting into the dark. He turned around once to wave, and then he was gone. When Andy turned back to go inside, he noticed that his cheeks were wet.

166

The next day was Boxing Day, and his aunt and uncle gave him a box of beer from Uncle Hugh's brewery. The box was a twelve-bottle carton with *Bricker's Brewery* and *India Pale Ale* printed in red and yellow and green on its sides and top. The box sat on the kitchen table.

"That's for me? Beer?" asked Andy.

"It is," said Uncle Hugh gravely.

Andy opened it and saw the puppy. It was black-and-white and it was lying in the otherwise empty box looking up at him with moist brown eyes. "A puppy!" cried Andy. "For me?" The pup was thin and undernourished and looked too young to have left its mother. It tried to stand, but the sight of Andy's astonished face caused it to tumble backwards in confusion.

His aunt and uncle said nothing but stood looking pleased with themselves.

For Andy it was love at first sight. He lifted the puppy carefully out of the box and let it hang helplessly in his hand. Mostly black, it had white legs, chest, and throat, with a narrow band of white running along the length of its nose up to the top of its head, leaving the eyes black, so that the face looked like a mask.

"I can't believe it! If you knew how long I've waited for a pup just like this! He's beautiful, he's exactly what I wanted. Thanks, Uncle Hugh! Thanks, Aunt Mona!"

His aunt and uncle continued to look pleased with themselves.

Andy thought for a second. "Is he a he?"

Uncle Hugh grinned. "He's a he. About three weeks old."

Andy held him up in the air. Tiny pink tongue, tiny black silky ears. He cradled the pup in his hands.

Aunt Mona snapped, "He's your responsibility now. You will have to take care of him, feed him, teach him how to behave. Can't have him doing his business all over the house. Otherwise he will have to go."

"Don't worry. I'll take care of him all right, I really will. He's perfect! Thanks for getting him for me. Don't worry, Aunt Mona, he'll be no trouble to you, I promise." He put the pup down on the kitchen floor and kneeled beside him, tickling and stroking and talking to him, but the poor thing was so young and weak he could barely move. He would be fine once he'd put on a little weight, Uncle Hugh said. Andy lay on his back, the pup on his chest, and looked up at his uncle. "What kind is he?"

Uncle Hugh pulled a face. "A mixture, I'd say. The mother was a mixture, but he's border collie mostly, by the look of him; belonged to one of the men at the brewery. This one is the runt of a litter of five, and the last to find a home."

"Will I be able to go see the mother sometimes?" asked Andy. "So I can take the pup and show her?"

Aunt Mona bit her lip.

Uncle Hugh's face flushed. He sent Aunt Mona an awkward glance.

"The mother's name was Trixie," he explained to Andy. "She was run over by a brewery truck on Christmas Eve, before her pups were ready to leave." He held up a baby bottle. "You'll need to feed him from the bottle for a while, a couple of weeks or so maybe."

168

"Warm milk," said Aunt Mona. "I'll help you with the bottle."

Andy looked at the pup sprawled weakly on his tiny chest and stroked his smooth coat with two fingers. No mother. We're the same, you and me, he thought. He noticed again the name on the beer box: *Bricker's Brewery.* He spoke the name aloud. "Bricker. Do you think that might be a good name for him?" He looked up at his uncle.

Uncle Hugh smiled. "Bricker's a good name."

"Then that's what I'll call him," Andy said happily. "Brick for short."

21

THERE WAS NO CALL from Vinny on the Sunday following the dinner. Andy was itching to tell him about Brick, so was doubly disappointed when he didn't phone. Nor was there a call on New Year's Day. Then it was back to school. School in Halifax wasn't very different from school in Vancouver, but already Vancouver seemed to Andy a distant memory, another life lived in another time. He missed nothing of Vancouver. Except his mother; he still thought of her often, as a finger finds a sore, worried, wondering where she was, a constant scab inside him.

This coming into a new school just before Christmas had aroused much interest and curiosity among the other kids. But now he found himself accepted. He had already put his name down for the soccer team. Many of the boys wore Moosehead shirts. One of them, John Bowman, crazy about hockey, was amazed that Andy had never played, and offered to coach him. There was lots of equipment at the school, he said.

Already Brick, stronger and healthier, was starting to

show an interest in his surroundings. Andy joined the library and borrowed a book on dog training. He and his uncle shopped for puppy things: a rubber bone to chew on, a collar and a leash, food, special vitamins. Soon Brick would need shots.

At home, Andy helped with Gran now, walking her to the downstairs toilet and helping her back again. Sometimes it took the two of them, Andy and Aunt Mona, to support her, for Gran's leg muscles were deteriorating from lack of use, though some days were better for her than others. On her good days she was bossy and noisy, demanding attention, and could hobble on Andy's arm without any trouble. Brick followed awkwardly, dodging their feet. But on her off days Gran dozed in front of the TV, and even when awake seemed insensible to most of what was going on around her. Her doctor said she should walk around the house for exercise, but she didn't like it and wouldn't do it, protesting loudly if Aunt Mona tried to make her.

"She seems to like me," Andy said to Aunt Mona one afternoon after school. "Maybe I could walk her about a bit; what do you think?"

"You can try if you like, but unless it's the toilet she wants, she'll scream at you, wait and see."

But Gran didn't scream at him. Andy and Brick walked her a few times around the small living room through the clutter of furniture, out to the hallway, around the potted aspidistra in her parlor bedroom, back to the hall, out to the kitchen, then back to her chair in front of the TV, Andy holding her under the elbow, taking some of her weight as she wobbled feebly along, imagining he was like a gas pump, pouring some of his own strength into her. Gran collapsed into her chair with a sigh at the end of it all. "Twice a day, Gran," Andy told her. "We'll do it twice a day, and as you get stronger we can try increasing the distance, okay?"

"I'm too old for all this running about, Andy," Gran whimpered. "My legs hurt."

"Wonders'll never cease," said Aunt Mona afterward.

"What's a word that means both 'space vehicle' and 'pill,' beginning with a c and ending with an e?" Uncle Hugh had started involving Andy in his evening struggles.

"How many letters?"

"Seven."

Andy thought hard. "How about 'capsule'?"

"That's it, Andy. Thanks."

Andy and Aunt Mona and Brick — who had his own special bowl — were eating breakfast together on a Tuesday morning in the middle of January. Uncle Hugh had already gone to work and Gran was still in bed. Aunt Mona said, "I got this letter yesterday. It's from the lawyer in Vancouver, about your stepfather's estate."

Andy listened. His aunt, reading glasses perched on the end of her nose, explained that "estate" meant what had been left in his mother's and stepfather's will, and that everything was to come to Andy in trust.

"What's 'in trust' mean?"

"Nobody can touch it. It's normal. The money from their bank accounts and from insurance and from the government flood relief fund will stay in the bank gathering interest until you're eighteen. Then you can do what you like with it."

"How much is there?"

Aunt Mona showed him the letter.

"That's a lot of money!"

"Not so very much. But with the interest it will be enough to start you off in life, pay for your education perhaps, if you decide to go to college."

"Can't I spend any of it now?"

"Not a penny. Nobody can touch that money, not even yourself who owns it, for seven years."

"That doesn't seem right. You spend money on me, and you need things here."

"Nothing is needed here," she snapped, standing abruptly. "Help me clear away the dishes." She pointed to the clock. "Lookit! You'll be late for school if you don't move yourself."

He helped with the dishes and then pulled on his parka and his boots. "See you later," he yelled into the kitchen, ready to fly out the door, Brick bouncing excitedly about his feet.

"Don't forget your lunch," Aunt Mona yelled back.

Andy grabbed his lunch bag off the sideboard, crammed it into his bag, and turned to run. "G'bye, Brick, see you later." But Brick didn't respond, for he was busy chasing his tail, something he'd just started doing lately; he ran around in circles, barking happily, as if trying to bite some imaginary tormentor.

"Wait! Let me look at you." Aunt Mona came hurrying from the kitchen, drying her hands on a tea towel.

"I'm late!" Andy protested. "Una's waiting for me."

Aunt Mona made a quick inspection of Andy's boots, pulled his parka down at the back, and fussed rapidly with his hair. "You need a haircut. Don't go racing across the road. Watch out for traffic. Don't be late home."

And he was gone.

He walked home from school with Una and John Bowman and a few others who lived in the same direction.

"Are you looking forward to living with your father?" Una asked him when only she and Andy were left and the other kids had gone their different ways.

"Of course. But I'll miss my aunt and uncle. And Gran."

"When will your father send for you, do you think?"

Andy looked up at dark gray banks of cloud massing over the houses. "I'm not sure. Soon, I expect." He didn't mention that Vinny hadn't phoned.

Una said, "Uncle Hugh and Aunt Mona are good people."

"Are you saying my father isn't a good person?"

"No, I am not saying that at all. Don't get angry for nothing."

"You've heard your mum and dad talking, haven't you? About my father. What do they say?"

"It's nothing, just that your father is used to living alone. And he's away a lot. You'd be on your own sometimes — "

"You're talking about him going to jail, aren't you? Well, he's finished with all that. He's getting a job soon — "

"The swings are empty," said Una. "Let's sit a minute."

"It looks like it's going to pour."

"Let's live dangerously, Andy, in the wild, remember? Come on."

They sat idly swinging while the air grew still and cold about them and the clouds gathered black and menacing over their heads.

"Andy? Promise you won't get mad at me if I ask you something."

"Like what?"

"Promise first."

Andy shrugged. "Okay."

"What if your dad doesn't send for you? And you have to stay with Aunt Mona."

Andy didn't want to think. "I don't know, Una."

A few spots of rain. "That's enough danger. Let's go," Una yelled, slipping off the swing and running, "before we get soaked."

When he got home, he found Gran asleep in front of the TV with the *Oprah* show on too loud and Aunt Mona rattling her broom about the kitchen. Brick followed him up the stairs to his room; he needed to be alone for a while to think about Una's unsettling question. He lay on the bed,

Brick prancing about beside him, and stared at the cracks on the ceiling, broken eggshell patterns he was coming to know so well.

"What if your dad doesn't ..."

He stared around the room. He used to hate it, but now ... He hadn't noticed until recently, but the wardrobe he'd thought ugly was actually very old, with fine carving around the edges of the set-in mirror, and was finished in a deep burnt-red polish ... Some of his books and papers were stacked in the wardrobe; others were piled on the chest ... The lemon wallpaper with the white butterflies, picked out by his aunt, made him think of spring when he woke every morning in the big bed ... It was a good room ... he liked it. And he'd made it his own, with schoolbooks and clothes and a few posters: pinup Mia Hamm of the U.S. women's soccer team; Ronaldo of Brazil; Wayne Gretzky.

What if your dad doesn't ...

Brick had his own box for sleeping, right beside Andy's bed, though more often than not he ended up sleeping on the bed with his master, which was one part of the training that wasn't working too well. But he had put on weight and was livelier, too lively sometimes, and was learning fast.

"What if your dad ..."

He rolled off the bed and went to the window, open at the top for fresh air. Brick stood alertly on the bed, watching to see where Andy would move next. The storm was gathering itself. Andy looked over the roofs of the houses at the black sky.

Down in the neighboring backyards Mrs. Fahey and

Mrs. O'Mahoney, neighbors he had come to know, were enjoying a shouted conversation as they raced the rain, snatching the washing off their lines and dropping clothespins and washing into plastic baskets as fast as they could. The rain started with a gust of cold air and a rush, and it pelted down hard. Andy grinned as Mrs. Fahey and Mrs. O'Mahoney, caught in the downpour, decided to save what they had and make a run for their back doors, screaming at the sky like gulls. Mrs. Fahey tripped and stumbled, tumbling her basket of clean clothes onto the slushy snow. Mrs. O'Mahoney's trailing bedsheet caught on the handlebar of her husband's rusty bicycle leaning against the wall dividing the two houses, and she stopped to disentangle it. Andy heard the sound of someone's wind chimes as the two women recovered themselves, gathered their soiled wash, and disappeared into their houses.

He stayed at the window for a while watching the rain, thinking about Vinny.

He is sleepy but can't sleep.

The rain stopped several hours ago, and now a gibbous moon sails high behind webs of cloud.

Thoughts and images keep up a slow drip in his head and he can't turn them off.

He thinks about his mother.

He worries about Vinny climbing down the broken fire escape, worries about Fingers Agostino coming after Vinny with a long sharp knife, worries about the police throwing his father in prison.

A tracery of cracks, the ones on the ceiling above the window, form a pair of faces in profile, joined together so that one looks out the window at the stars, and the other faces the opposite way at the blank wall. Like Janus, the two-faced god of beginnings. Andy remembers Janus because of January, the month that looks back at the old year and forward to the new. He has never noticed the ceiling faces in the daylight; they're a trick of silver moonlight and black shadows.

The next day he came home from school to find Aunt Mona washing vegetables at the kitchen sink and asked her if she needed a hand. She told him to go do his homework, as she usually did: schoolwork was more important than kitchen work, she always said.

Brick jumped up on him, desperate for his attention. Andy didn't ask his aunt if his father had called because he already knew the answer. He lingered, crouching to pet Brick. "Maybe on Saturday I'll visit my father."

Aunt Mona said nothing, but lifted a shoulder in a tiny shrug.

"He'll call eventually, I'm sure, when he gets a job."

His aunt said nothing.

"Don't you think?"

Her lips tightened. She turned off the running water.

Andy said, "It was good of you and Uncle Hugh to have me here all this time — while we're waiting, I mean."

Aunt Mona nodded her head without looking up from her task. "Judith was my sister. I'm not one to shirk my duty."

Duty. Andy felt his stomach lurch. "Isn't a duty something you must do even if you don't want to? Like … like washing dishes?"

Aunt Mona dropped what she was doing, dried her hands hastily on a towel, and turned quickly to glare at him, hands on hips. "You've the quick tongue, Andy Flynn. You take me wrong. I'm thankful to God for such a duty. Haven't we been praying to the Blessed Virgin every day for your peace of mind, praying you'll settle happy here with us!" She turned back to the sink with busy hands.

Silence.

Then she said, "Hugh would miss you terrible if you left us."

"What about you, Aunt Mona? Would you miss me terrible, too?"

She did not answer but became very still. Then she said to the tiny kitchen window in front of her, "After you ran off … in the bus station … I cried. Destroyed with the pain of it I was. Someone helped me to a seat. To this day I don't remember who it was, man, woman, or child." She tried to say more, but her voice failed her.

Andy waited in silence.

Then, quietly emphatic, Aunt Mona said, "Would I miss you? Of *course* I would miss you!"

Andy stared at her stiff back, then saw her shoulders loosen.

With a catch in her voice, she said again softly, "I would miss you, Andy. I'd be desperate, and that's the truth." She turned to him, her eyes wet with tears.

Brick barked at Andy for attention.

"You had better go up and do your homework," whispered Aunt Mona.

Andy grabbed Brick and carried him up the stairs to his room.

22

ON SATURDAY AFTERNOON he went to the hockey game with John and a bunch of the other kids. The Mooseheads were at home to the Moncton Wildcats. Andy and his friends high-fived the players as they came onto the ice. The Mooseheads won. It was a good game. "Do the hockey pucks always disappear like that, during a game, and they have to bring on new ones?" Andy asked his friends.

Thinking of Vinny.

Lying in his bed, Sunday morning early, listening to the sounds of the house, then Hugh's quiet tread on the stair bringing Mona tea in bed, then Mona up and rattling about the kitchen. Lying in bed, Brick beside him but eager to go downstairs, staring at the cracks and thinking of Vinny. Vinny and Judith dancing the whole night through — I missed you something dreadful, Andy, it's brilliant you're here — astonished to see you — a new purpose now — a fine young man you are — not easy to raise a young boy, but don't worry, leave it to me — take good care of you

— promise — leave it to me — promise — leave it to me
— to me —

Vinny won't change. Vinny with his stale cigarettes and whiskey, his songs and jokes, his gambling. Vinny with his moonlight and raisins and thorn trees. A lion in the wild, Vinny will never change. Andy is beginning to understand that now. Vinny is Vinny. Just as Mona is Mona and Hugh is Hugh. Vinny will never find a job, Andy now realizes. Or move from the Mayo Rooms. Or change his life. It isn't possible to change Vinny, no matter how hard Andy tries. What did Vinny say when Andy warned him about smoking? "I'm too old to give it up. Set in my ways I am." No, only Vinny can change Vinny, nobody else. The thought strikes Andy with the force of a blow.

He slides out of bed and looks out the window. Brick is already at the door, impatient to be let out. Sunshine. Lots to do today: go get John after mass and kick the ball around with the other kids, get a game going maybe. He can't wait. He dresses quickly, skips downstairs, and lets Brick out the back door into the yard. He feels good. Better than good; he feels great. "Grand," as Vinny would say.

He feels free.

Uncle Hugh is in the living room reading a Sunday paper. He looks up. "Good morning, Andy." Grand smile.

"It's a grand day, Uncle."

His aunt is still in the kitchen, making porridge and mixing batter for pancakes. Andy has already changed his mind about porridge; his aunt's tastes better than his

182

mother's. "Let me do that, Aunt Mona; I'm grand at stirring porridge."

"Grand is it? Very well." She leaves the porridge for him to finish. "You sound chipper this morning. Must be the sunshine." She mixes the batter.

"Big soccer game today."

"Soccer is it? Then maybe you should be playing every day if that's how happy you'd be."

Aunt Mona has a nice face when she smiles, Andy decides.

Uncle Hugh appears at the kitchen door, newspaper trailing in his hand. Andy can tell by the grin on his face he has been listening. He and Aunt Mona exchange glances.

"A grand morning," Hugh says, his face stiff and serious.

"Grand altogether," Mona agrees, nodding, hiding a smile.

Monday, after school. He gave the secret knock and waited. Then he tried the door; locked; Vinny out. Or not home yet, more like.

He'd remembered to bring his key this time.

The place looked exactly the same. He hadn't realized just how poor and bare and cold it really was. A spoonful of raisins in the saucer. Vinny and his raisins. No changes except the *Playboy* centerfold back on the wall near the kitchen.

The place smelled stale; he'd forgotten about the smell.

Vinny would never change. Somehow that seemed okay now; Andy accepted the idea that people could change only themselves, not others. He lay on the sofa, stretching himself out in this new freedom of understanding. The flood had claimed his mother's life, he accepted that now; someone you loved could die; his mother was dead. The flood had killed his mother and had tossed him, upside down, into the arms of a tree. But now he was back on his feet, no longer upside down, seeing the world the right way up, the way things really were, recognizing his father's weakness and his aunt's strength.

By nine o'clock he was cold and restless. He wished he'd told Aunt Mona he was coming over. He should get back and save her worrying. He got up and opened the window and looked out. No rain and an almost full moon. The fire escape hadn't been fixed. He looked in the fridge. The usual: milk and tea and raisins and an opened packet of potato chips. He stayed away from the bedroom, resisting an urge to look under the bed.

At ten o'clock he walked over to Dan Noonan's. Vinny wasn't there.

He tried Ryan's and the Pink Elephant: no Vinny. He walked back to the Mayo and knocked in case his father had returned, then let himself in and lay on the sofa again, covering himself with a blanket.

A moonbeam shone through the window, bathing the raisins on the table in a pale silver glow.

He would wait for as long as it took, even if Vinny didn't come home till morning.

He fell asleep.

The sound of the key rattling in the lock woke him up. He looked at his new watch. Past midnight.

"Andy, is it you?" Vinny surprised.

Andy sat up. He could see that his father had been drinking: slow, tired movements, strong smell of the pub. "Hi, Dad."

Vinny collapsed into the chair without taking off his old raincoat, its pockets empty. "What are you doing here? Did you run away from your aunt again?"

"I didn't run away."

"You came to see your poor old father."

"Yes. I worry about you, Dad, I worry that you're all right. You promised to call, so when you don't call I imagine the worst, that you've fallen off the fire escape again, or that Fingers Agostino and his sidekick have hurt you."

His father snorted. "Those two thicks! It's nice you worry about me, Andy darlin', but I'm used to looking after myself."

"Also, Dad, I need to ask you if it's okay for me to stay with Aunt Mona and Uncle Hugh. And Gran. We get along, and I'm used to the school and everything, so I'd like to stay where I am. For now anyway. If that's all right with you."

His father stared at him, surprised.

Andy said, "You wouldn't need to move from here if you didn't want to. You could stay, and we'd still see each other, lots. But I just wanted you to know I'm okay where I am right now and you shouldn't worry about me and you needn't worry about moving, like I said."

His father grinned. He looked relieved. "Maybe that's best, Andy, for a wee while anyway, till the job situation improves and I can find a place for us. Meantime, your aunt can do more for you than I can and that's the truth. And Hughie's a Galway man, so you can't go wrong there. But I'll come over and see you regular, leave it to me. I'll keep an eye on you, don't you fret about that." He nodded his head several times. "Don't you fret about that," he said again. "Would you like a cup of tea to warm you?"

"No thanks, I've got to get back. It's late and there's school tomorrow."

There was a soft knock on the door, uncoded.

Vinny struggled up and opened the door a few inches, keeping a foot behind it.

"Hello, Vincent."

Aunt Mona, stern and haughty as usual.

Vinny opened the door wider. "It's yourself. Come in, Mona, come in."

"I won't come in. It's late. I came for Andy."

Andy went to his aunt.

Vinny said, "I'll be here if you need me, Andy, don't forget."

"No, Dad, I won't forget. I'll come to see you the Saturday after next, in the morning, late, have a cup of tea with you, make sure you're okay. I'll bring Brick — he's my dog, a puppy — so you can meet him."

Vinny gave a tired smile and ruffled Andy's hair affectionately. "That'll be lovely."

Andy descended the stairs to the street with his aunt

and they stood together at the bus stop. The street was flooded with moonlight, and the tops of the trees whispered together in the wind, sharing secrets.

His aunt said, "It was so late. We were worried. You okay?"

"I'm okay," said Andy, and he was. He looked up at his aunt. "I told him I wanted to stay with you and Hugh and Gran."

Aunt Mona smiled and nodded.

Andy said, "Do you think he'll be all right? Without me, I mean?"

"He'll be fine."

"Do you remember you told me that my father is wasting his life?"

"I do."

"Well, I don't think it's wasted. He's happy. He's got lots of friends, people who love him. And he's got me. I don't think it's wasted, Aunt Mona."

Mona thought for a few seconds. Then she said, "You're a fine boy, Andy. Your father's proud of you, anyone can see that."

They looked along the bright, empty street.

"The last bus has gone," said Mona.

"Then we'll walk," said Andy, taking his aunt's thin arm.

They set off together, walking through the moonlit streets while what was left of the summer's dry leaves rose up in tiny whirlwinds about their feet and the Sheehogue danced happily behind them all the way home.

Air Canada, flight 185, Halifax to Vancouver.

The Old One was exhausted. He slept almost the whole way home.

The Young Ones celebrated their freedom in a harmless exuberance of broken rules, causing tiny problems with teapots, coffee urns, and meal trays; flight attendants warned everyone to watch out for hockey pucks skating down the aisle; a washroom door had to be forced open to release an extremely large lady who was yelling to be let out; the dialogue of the American in-flight movie came through, without subtitles, in a strange language that one scholarly passenger swore was ancient Celtic. On arrival in Vancouver, the crew agreed that it had been an abnormal flight, not simply because of the strange incidents and unusually high number of minor accidents, but mainly because of the merry good spirits of their passengers.